T-2

Drifter

When El Carcinero and his outlaw gang raided the Mercer ranch, they turned life upside-down for young Emily Mercer, who was away at school at the time.

The mystery man known as Drifter was an old friend of the Mercers. But much as he wanted to get even with El Carcinero, he just didn't see how it was possible. Aside from the fact that he'd be hopelessly outgunned, the bandits had long-since fled back across the border into Mexico. Still, he hadn't reckoned on Emily. Wise beyond her years, she was determined to get back the horses the outlaws had stolen – especially her beloved stallion, Diablo – and no one was going to stop her.

So she and a lawman, well past his prime, rode out after the bandits. Since Drifter couldn't let them go by themselves, he went right along too. And when the gun-swift Mesquite Jennings joined their small army, he almost started to feel sorry for El Carcinero. Almost. . . .

Drifter

Steve Hayes

A Black Horse Western

ROBERT HALE · LONDON

ISBN 978-0-7090-9629-0

Robert Hale Limited
Clerkenwell House
Clerkenwell Green
London EC1R 0HT

www.halebooks.com

Typeset by
Derek Doyle & Associates, Shaw Heath
Printed and bound in Great Britain by
CPI Antony Rowe, Chippenham and Eastbourne

For Borden and Frank Chase
Western writers extraordinaire
Thanks for your friendship

CHAPTER ONE

Sheriff Lonnie Forbes sat slumped in his old rocking chair on the boardwalk fronting his office, long legs stretched out before him, contentedly smoking his customary after-dinner cigar. From here he could see everything that was happening on both sides of Main Street, a broad, unpaved, former stagecoach and wagon trail that ran string-straight through the hot dusty town of Santa Rosa, New Mexico.

A tall, big-bellied, fleshy man with a face like a mottled cauliflower, he was on the wrong side of sixty and gray side-burns showed under the brim of his pulled-down Stetson. His drooping mustache was also gray, but the hairs close to his lips were stained brown by snuff. He was known to occasionally accept bribes, but even his enemies admitted that most of the time he was an honest lawman who, though inherently lazy, upheld the law and felt secure in the knowledge that no one had run against him in five years.

A mosquito whined near his ear. He blew smoke at it, chasing it away, then clasped his hands across his silver-and-turquoise belt buckle and closed his weary hazel eyes. As he began to doze off, he contemplated whether to cross the street and have a beer at Rosario's Cantina or stroll down to the Widow Sylvia's on Oak Street and enjoy a wedge of her famous cinnamon-apple pie that had won last year's pie-eating contest.

7

Before he could decide, he heard horses approaching. The crisp mile-consuming trot and jingling of sabers told him it was the cavalry before he even opened his eyes.

He was right. Led by former West Point graduate, Lt. James Ellesworth, the patrol rode past the stock yards and entered town, their uniforms and horses caked with sweat and dust.

Sheriff Forbes sighed, irked that his peaceful evening was about to be interrupted. Rising, he leaned against the hitch-rail and watched as the column of twos rode out of the twilight toward him.

They were escorting a wagon driven by a man the sheriff had never seen before. Tall, whip-lean, and tanned from years in the saddle, he had hawkish features and fierce gray eyes that exuded independence. He was hatless, and a blood-stained bandage was tied around his shaggy, unkempt black hair. He wore a sun-faded denim shirt and blue, Union-cavalry pants tucked into Apache knee-high moccasins. Tied to the rear of the wagon was his horse, a rangy long-legged sorrel with a blond mane and tail that looked as wild and free as the man who owned him.

Sensing trouble, the lawman wondered who the man was and what he'd done to warrant a military escort.

The patrol now reined up before him. The troopers were as weary as their horses, and by Lt. Ellesworth's grim expression, the sheriff knew that his news was bad.

' 'Evenin', Lieutenant.'

'Sheriff . . .' Lt. Ellesworth dismounted, slapped the trail dust from his blue uniform with his hat, and mounted the boardwalk. Shaking the sheriff's hand, he said: ' 'Fraid I got bad news. A bunch of Comancheros crossed the border this morning and raided two ranches. The survivors couldn't give us an exact count, but most figured it was around twenty riders.'

Sheriff Forbes spat his disgust into the street. 'And I'll

wager they're led by that no-good 'breed, *El Carnicero.*'

'You'd win that wager.'

'They headed this way?'

'I've no idea where they're headed, though back to Mexico seems the most logical place.'

'Who were the victims?'

'Old Man Tabor and a cowhand, whom we buried, and the Mercers,' the lieutenant said gravely. 'Found them all scalped and murdered—'

'The Mercers are *dead?*'

'Father, mother, and both sons.'

Sheriff Forbes sagged. 'Sonofa*bitch,*' he said after a shocked silence.

'I know they're friends of yours—'

'Mine – and just about everyone else around these parts.'

'Lonnie, I'm truly sorry—'

The sheriff wasn't listening. 'Hell, I was talkin' to Frank just the day 'fore yesterday. Bumped into him comin' out of Melvin's Mercantile and he insisted on buyin' me a goddamn beer . . .' his voice trailed off.

There was a grim, awkward silence.

Lt. Ellesworth shifted uncomfortably on his feet. 'I . . . uh . . . wasn't sure what to do with the bodies. Normally I would've had a detail bury them at the ranch, like I did with Old Man Tabor. But according to that fella, there,' he thumbed at the wagon on which the man sat, blank-faced and motionless, 'the daughter's away at some fancy boarding school in Las Cruces and would definitely want to be here when they're put in the ground.'

'He's right,' Sheriff Forbes said. 'Miss Emily's been gone since right after Christmas. Who the hell is he, anyway?'

'I don't know. We found him at the ranch. He'd been hit on the head and was still groggy. Thought at first he was a half-breed – maybe even one of the Comancheros. But turns out he's white as I am.'

'He got a name?'

'Drifter.'

'Drifter? What the hell kinda name is that?'

Lt. Ellesworth shrugged. 'It's all I could get out of him.'

'I've known Frank Mercer for almost fifteen years and I ain't never heard him mention no one by that name.'

'Maybe not. But my guess is he's telling the truth. I mean, if they weren't acquainted, then how'd he know about the daughter being away?'

'Good question,' Sheriff Forbes said sourly. 'And one I intend to get an answer to pretty goddamn *quick*.'

A crowd had gathered around the wagon. Someone pulled back the blood-stained tarp covering the Mercers. The gory sight of the butchered, scalped bodies made the women gasp and turn away, sickened. The men, outraged, began taking their anger out on Drifter.

He ignored them. But his tight-lipped, jut-jawed expression showed he was boiling inside.

The sheriff, worried things might get out of control, quickly intervened. 'Get down, mister,' he told Drifter. 'Go wait for me in my office.'

'Not till I turn the bodies over to the undertaker.'

'I'll take care of that. Now do like I say. Pronto!'

Drifter didn't move. His gray eyes stared fixedly at the lawman.

'Ask me politely,' he said. He had a faint Texas drawl and spoke as if he'd been educated. 'Then I'll consider it.'

Sheriff Forbes almost choked. He was tempted to reach for his six-gun, but something about the man warned him not to press the issue.

'Be obliged if you'd talk to me in my office, *hombre*.'

'Soon as I've grained my horse,' Drifter promised. He rubbed his nose with his fist, a habit he'd acquired over the years. Then tying the reins around the brake-handle, he grabbed his 45-70 caliber Winchester '86 from the seat,

10

jumped down, and untied his horse. The sorrel nipped at him, causing Drifter to jump back and curse softly. He then led the horse across the street to Lars Gustafson's livery stable.

One of the men in the crowd belligerently confronted the sheriff. 'How come you let that murderin' 'breed walk away?'

Immediately, others angrily demanded to know the same thing.

Sheriff Forbes held up a meaty hand, silencing everyone. 'All right, that's enough,' he barked. 'All of you – you got no business here. Go home.'

'We ain't goin' anywhere,' the man said defiantly. 'Not till we find out what you intend to do about that goddamn 'breed.'

'Herb,' Sheriff Forbes said quietly, 'first off, he ain't a 'breed. Second, I'm the law in Santa Rosa and I've been the law here long 'fore your daddy died and left you rich enough to think you're goddamn important.'

Herb Truex flushed, embarrassed. 'Got no call to talk to me like that, Lonnie. I voted for you.'

'You *voted* for J.J. Saunders and we both know it. But no matter. You don't like how I'm handlin' things, Herb, you can always run agin me come election time. In fact I'd look forward to it. Meanwhile, I've given you an order and you better damn well obey it. All of you! Clear the street. Go on,' he said as no one moved. 'Go back to your homes. Tend to your families. If the Comancheros are still around and do hit us, what happened to Old Man Tabor the Mercers could easily happen to you.'

Grumbling, the crowd began to disperse.

But Sheriff Forbes could see their rage against Drifter was still escalating. Worried that they might change their minds and try to lynch him, he turned to Lt. Ellesworth, saying: 'Maybe you and your men ought to stick around 'case I need you.'

'Sorry. My orders are to track down the hostiles and take them back to the fort.'

'I'll remind you 'bout your orders if they string him up.'

'Talk like that,' said Lt. Ellesworth, stepping up into the saddle, 'makes me think maybe it's time you retired.'

Immune to sarcasm, Sheriff Forbes said, 'Some folks 'round here think I'm already retired.' Then as the lieutenant chuckled: 'When you file your report, Jim, mention that I'm wirin' Miss Emily 'bout her folks, so she can tell me how she wants to handle the funeral.'

'Will do,' Lt. Ellesworth said. He saluted goodbye. Then, motioning for his men to follow, he led them toward the public drinking trough to water their horses.

'Hang on to your hair,' Sheriff Forbes called after him.

CHAPTER TWO

The small, sparsely furnished office was divided in half by a wall on which were pinned a row of wanted posters. One of them offered a thousand dollar reward, dead or alive, for the outlaw Mesquite Jennings. Beside it was a barred door leading to the cells. Flies buzzed in the dusky heat, their tiny bodies bumping against the unwashed windows. Everything reeked of stale coffee and dead cigars.

The sheriff went to the pot-bellied stove in the corner and filled his mug with muddy-looking coffee. He looked up as Drifter entered, then pointed to another mug and said: 'Help yourself.'

Drifter looked disparagingly at the coffee and shook his head.

Sheriff Forbes grinned. 'What don't kill you only makes you stronger.'

'Thanks. I'll pass.'

The sheriff flopped down behind his desk, motioned for Drifter to sit across from him, and studied the man over the rim of his mug. 'Soon as we're done, I'll walk you over to Doc Chandler. Have him fix you up.'

'Army's already done that.'

'Suit yourself. Now,' the sheriff said, lighting the chewed stub of a Mexican cigar, 'I need you to tell me exactly what went on out at the Mercers. And don't leave one goddamn word out.'

'You saw the bodies, Sheriff. What else is there to tell?'

'Your part in it, for starters.'

Drifter thought a moment, his expression blank. 'They hit just before sunset,' he said finally. 'Came in fast, on foot and from all sides—'

'So they caught you by surprise?'

'Didn't say that.'

'Go on.'

'I'd heard them signaling to each other in the mesquite. They wanted us to think it was quail but I could tell the difference. I warned the Mercers and by the time the attack came we were all in the house, ready for them.'

Sheriff Forbes frowned, puzzled. 'Frank Mercer built that house more'n a decade ago. He built the sonofabitch real solid, walls thick as a fort, knowin' he might have to fight off Apaches and Comanches, which were still on the prod then.'

'I know,' Drifter said. He rubbed his nose with his fist, adding: 'Years ago, when I first watered my horse there, Frank told me how it used to be back in the seventies.'

'Then maybe *you'd* like to tell me, mister, how come five of you – armed with Colts an' Winchesters – couldn't hold off a bunch of Comancheros?'

'We did hold them off – till we had nothing left to hold them off with.'

'Mean you run out of ammo?'

Drifter nodded.

'You wanna chew that again?'

'No need.'

'In other words, you're sure about it?'

Again Drifter nodded.

'See, reason I ask is, I saw Frank in town two days ago. Happened to ask him where his boys were and he said they were over at Denson's pickin' up the ammo he'd ordered.'

'So?'

'So unless you were usin' a Gatlin gun I don't know about, or were real careless with your shootin', how come you run out of ammo?'

'Spring cleanin'.'

'What?'

'Day before yesterday Martha – Mrs Mercer – had her husband and sons clear everything out of the house so she could do her spring cleaning. Pots and pans, furniture, stuff on the shelves, even some of the food in the pantry; they piled it all in the barn. Then, that night when she was finished, they carried mostly everything back in the house—'

'But not the ammo, that the fish story you're tryin' to hook me with?'

'I'm not trying to hook you, period,' Drifter said. 'That's how it was.'

Sheriff Forbes drained his coffee and relit his cigar. 'Go on,' he said finally. 'Button up your story.'

'When the Comancheros attacked the first time, we managed to drive them off. Frank knew they'd be back and said we most likely couldn't stop them from stealing the mares, but we had to save the stallion so he'd be able to keep on breeding once they bought new stock. Diablo was in the barn and I suggested we bring him into the house, where he'd be safe.'

'What about the ammo?'

'It was still in the barn. But no one remembered that till after they hit us again. Then Frank, knowing we couldn't hold them off for long with what few rounds we had, told us to cover him while he went and got it. But he was limping so badly from his gout I figured he probably wouldn't make it there and back, so I went instead.'

'You risked your life for strangers?'

'The Mercers aren't strangers. I've been watering my horse there for many summers, and Martha's always insisted

I stay over for supper.'

'Funny, Frank's never mentioned you. Martha, neither.'

'Why would they? I'm just a saddle-bum drifting through.'

Sheriff Forbes didn't believe that, but let it slide for now. 'That reminds me. The lieutenant says you told him your name was Drifter.'

'It's as good as any.'

'Been my experience that a fella who won't tell his real name usually has somethin' to hide.'

'When you figure out what it is,' Drifter said pleasantly, 'let me know.'

The sheriff let that slide too. 'What happened after you got to the barn?'

'Two Comancheros had already broken in.' Drifter gingerly felt his bandaged head. 'One jumped me, while the other clubbed me from behind . . . that's all I remember.'

'That's mighty convenient.'

'Unless you're the one being clubbed.'

'Save your sarcasm for someone who 'preciates it,' Sheriff Forbes said. He sighed, troubled. 'So let me get this straight: these two Comancheros, they had a chance to scalp you an' never done it? Why you think that is?'

'Dunno.'

'Maybe they figured you're one of 'em?'

'Then why hit me at all?'

'Been askin' myself that and so far I ain't come up with an answer.'

'You suggesting I hit myself?'

'I ain't suggesting anythin'. Just tryin' to get to the truth. What about the Mercers,' the sheriff asked. 'Did you see 'em get killed?'

'Uh-uh. By the time I came around they were already dead and had their hair lifted.'

'And the hostiles, they'd ridden off?'

Drifter nodded.

'How long were you unconscious, y'think?'

'I don't know. Not long.'

'Long enough so you couldn't shoot none of your friends?'

'They're not my *friends*,' Drifter said.

'They're not your enemies either, or you'd be dead like the Mercers.'

'It's possible they thought I was dead.'

The sheriff eyed Drifter's long dark hair. 'Must've thought they'd scalped you, too.'

'Now who's being sarcastic.'

The sheriff muttered something unpleasant under his breath, then said: 'Thing I find mighty puzzlin' is why the Comancheros left in such a hurry.'

'Must've seen the troopers coming.'

'What makes you say that?'

'Because as I came out of the barn, Lt. Ellesworth and his men rode up.'

Sheriff Forbes had to admit the answer made sense. 'The ammo – what happened to it?'

'Comancheros took it – 'long with the mares and the stallion.'

That made sense too. The sheriff thought a moment, then rising, he took a Bible from his desk, returned and held it out flat to Drifter. 'You swear 'fore God Almighty that what you just told me is true and accurate?'

Without hesitation, Drifter placed his hand on the Bible. 'I do.'

'And there ain't no possible chance you could be mis-rememberin'?'

'No. Any *more* questions?'

'Reckon not,' Sheriff Forbes said, unconvinced. Returning the Bible to his desk drawer, he grabbed the cell keys from a hook near the gun-rack and motioned for

Drifter to follow him.

'You locking me up?'

'It's for your own safety, mister. Way you're dressed and that long hair of yourn has got folks convinced you're a 'breed who helped the Comancheros kill the Mercers. You go outside and pretty quick someone puts a bullet in you. Or you put one in them. Either way, my job's tough enough without invitin' any more damn trouble.'

Drifter looked at the keys, then at the cells beyond the barred door and quickly stepped back, his rifle covering the big lawman. 'Sorry,' he said. 'You might be right about the way folks are feeling right now, but I can't be locked up in a cell. Be worse than a bear caught in a trap.'

'Hell, it's only for one night,' the sheriff said. 'Come mornin', tempers will have cooled off and you can ride on out of here.'

Drifter didn't say anything but kept his rifle trained on the lawman.

'I'm warnin' you, mister,' said Forbes, 'Right about now, 'cross the street, that damn fool Truex is buyin' everybody free drinks, gettin' 'em all liquored up so he can talk 'em into a necktie party. I don't get over there soon and break things up, they'll turn into a mob – a mob I may not be able to stop, which means you'll end up dancin' from a rope. That what you want?'

Before Drifter could answer a rock crashed through the window, startling him and the sheriff. Shattered glass landed around their boots.

Drifter sighed, rubbed his nose with his fist and levered a shell into the chamber of his rifle. 'Reckon the decision's out of our hands,' he said quietly.

CHAPTER THREE

'Sheriff!' Truex yelled. 'Sheriff Forbes, you hear me?'

'I hear you, Herb.'

'Bring that stinking 'breed out here!'

'Go home, Herb,' Sheriff Forbes said. He took a double-barreled 20-gauge shotgun from the rack, made sure it was loaded, and went to the broken window. 'Same goes for the rest of you,' he shouted. 'You're breakin' the law! All of you! Go home!'

'We ain't goin' nowhere,' yelled another man. 'You don't bring that murderin' skunk out here right now, we're comin' in there to get him!'

'Got the same ten seconds you gave us,' Truex shouted. 'Then we're comin' in. Ten . . . nine . . .'

The sheriff sighed and rolled his eyes at Drifter. 'Knew you was trouble minute I laid eyes on you.'

Unfazed, Drifter said: 'Why not give them what they want?'

The sheriff frowned, for a moment not understanding. Then he smiled a thin tight smile that never reached his hazel eyes. 'Why not?' he said grimly. 'I've had it with this town anyways.' He moved to the window, shouting:

'We're comin' out!'

Outside, the mob gathered before the sheriff's office

19

grew tense with anticipation.

Truex mounted the boardwalk, faced the mob and brandished his rope at them. 'See?' he said drunkenly, 'what'd I tell you? Known Lonnie since we were young'uns. Always was a gutless bastard, an' always will be—'

He broke off, eyes popping, as the door swung open and Sheriff Forbes stepped out. Far from looking gutless, he stood tall and formidable, shotgun held down by his side, his free hand resting on his holstered six-gun.

'You want him,' he said to Truex, 'come an' take him.'

As he spoke Drifter emerged and stood beside the sheriff. Winchester in hand, he looked more than formidable; he looked deadly.

'Well, come on,' Sheriff Forbes said, addressing everyone but looking directly at Truex. 'Step up here an' take him.'

'Don't think we won't, neither,' Truex snarled.

'I don't,' the sheriff said. 'After all your loud-mouth yammerin', you don't take him now, why hell, all these folks are gonna know you for the fart-posturin', wind-suckin' blowhard you always been!'

Herb Truex whitened with rage. 'Damn you, Forbes,' he began.

He got no further as Drifter slammed him across the face with his rifle.

Truex staggered back, stunned, stumbled off the boardwalk, and fell to his knees.

Sheriff Forbes grinned at Drifter. '*Amigo*,' he said slowly, 'you took the words right out of my mouth.'

Truex, blood running from his nose and mouth, went for his gun.

Drifter snapped off one shot. Truex screamed and dropped his gun as the bullet punched a hole in his hand.

The mob froze, not sure how to react.

Sheriff Forbes pounced on their indecision. Leveling his shotgun at them, he taunted: 'Go ahead! Slap leather! See what it gets you!'

Then as no one moved:

'What the hell you waitin' for? You came here to see this fella dance from a rope – well, come ahead. Get on with it! 'Course, some of you ain't gonna live to see it, but what's that matter? You'll get your goddamn names in the news-paper. Make the obituaries. Even become part of local history.'

The mob shifted uneasily on its feet, their angry mutter-ings blending in with the tinkling piano music coming from the saloon opposite.

'Looks to me,' Sheriff Forbes told Truex, 'like you wasted your goddamn money liquorin' these folks up. Seems they don't have the belly for a lynchin', like you figured.'

'This ain't over,' Truex told Drifter and the sheriff. 'I'll make you pay for this. Both of you!'

'Lookin' forward to it,' Drifter drawled.

'Me, too,' said Sheriff Forbes. 'Meantime, Herb, bring me that rope.'

'Go to hell.'

The sheriff turned to Drifter. 'Reckon you can put a hole through his other hand?'

'Be happy to try,' Drifter said. Then to Truex: 'Hold still now. I don't want to miss and put one in your belly by mistake.'

'W-Wait. . . .' Truex staggered up and brought the rope to the sheriff.

The lawman smiled, tauntingly. 'Now that wasn't so hard, was it?'

Then as Truex's bloodshot eyes narrowed with fury:

'Tell you what, Herb. I'm gonna let this slide this time. But you ever try to take the law into your own hands again I'll let all the hot air out of your belly with buckshot. Clear?'

Truex nodded.

'Same goes for all of you,' the sheriff told the now-silent mob. 'Now, get out of my goddamn sight!'

CHAPTER FOUR

Just after sunup the next morning Sheriff Forbes woke Drifter, who was cat-napping in a chair in the office, and offered to buy him breakfast at the cantina across the street.

Drifter chuckled. 'Charitable are the guilty, they say.'

'Day I pinned on this star,' the sheriff replied testily, 'I done away with all thoughts of guilt an' charity. Now, you comin' or not?'

'On one condition.'

'Man, you sorely know how to test a fella's patience. OK, name it.'

'I go with you to meet Miss Emily on the morning train.'

'What makes you think she'll be on it?'

'Did you wire her 'bout her folks, like you told the lieutenant?'

'I did.'

'She'll be on it.'

Sheriff Forbes had already decided the same thing. He pondered a moment then said: 'I got your word you'll ride out right afterwards?'

Drifter gave a rare grin. 'Try to stop me.'

In an effort to show visitors that Santa Rosa was a neat, prosperous little town, every year the tiny, wood-framed station-house was repainted yellow with a chocolate-brown

23

trim. But within a few months the relentless desert winds and searing heat bleached out both colors until they looked almost the same, turning the building into a colorless, sand-pitted eyesore.

This morning there were several townspeople waiting for passengers arriving on the 9.18 from El Paso and points east. The train was already thirty minutes late and the sun hot enough to fry bacon, adding to the irritation of the folks waiting. On top of that, word of the Mercers' butchering had spread and as Sheriff Forbes and Drifter stepped on to the platform, the four men and two women gave them despising stares.

'Good thing the election isn't tomorrow,' Drifter said to the big lawman, 'or you'd be turning in your star.'

The sheriff spat disgustedly into the dust. 'To hell with 'em. Like I told the lieutenant, I'm 'bout ready to cash in anyway. Seems like no matter how hard you try to please, you tread on somebody's toes. You ever pinned on a badge?' he added, curious.

Drifter shook his head.

'There's worse ways to earn a dollar.'

'Name one.'

'Clerking . . . barkeep . . . punchin' cattle. . . .'

Drifter shrugged but said nothing.

'Ever done any of them things?'

'Nope.'

'What have you done, 'sides drift, I mean?'

For a moment it looked like Drifter was going to tell the sheriff to mind his own business. Then he said: 'Wrangler, mostly.'

'Breakin' broomtails? Ouch,' Sheriff Forbes winced. 'Now that's one tough way to earn a peso.'

'I dunno. 'Least horses don't jump to conclusions or try to hang you.'

'But they do stomp you. Ever work for Frank Mercer?'

'Uh-uh. But I doubt if a more honest or charitable boss ever lived.'

'Amen. An' Miss Emily's cut from the same cloth.' The sheriff squinted off along the tracks as the sound of a distant train whistle reached them on the wind. 'Leastwise, she was when she went off to school. But I reckon I ain't tellin' you nothin' you don't already know, right?'

Drifter ignored the question. Giving a troubled sigh, he said: 'I'd give a year of my life not to have to see her face when she steps off that train.'

Sheriff Forbes frowned at him. 'Yet you volunteered to come?'

'Sometimes you got to do the right thing,' Drifter said, 'no matter how painful.'

CHAPTER FIVE

Only four passengers got off the train. Emily Margaret Mercer was the last. Dressed entirely in mourning black, she waited for the conductor to set her two bags on the platform and then stood there, ladylike even at fourteen, her sad, dark eyes watching Sheriff Forbes and Drifter approaching. She was tall, slim, and just missed being an eyefull. She had lovely clear skin, thick lustrous brown hair, her mother's pert nose, and her father's smile. Today, though, she wasn't smiling and her eyes were red-raw from lack of sleep and crying.

Sheriff Forbes tipped his hat to her. ' 'Mornin', Miss Emily.'

'Good morning, Sheriff.' Emily nodded politely at Drifter, and then looked back at the lawman. 'Thank you for notifying me of my family's death . . . and also for coming to meet me.'

She conducted herself like a mature woman who seemed very much in control of her emotions. But Drifter heard acute pain in her voice and it twisted through him like barbed wire.

'Your pa was my friend,' the sheriff said. 'It's the least I could do. If you'll get the bags,' he added to Drifter, 'I'll escort Miss Emily into town. I took the liberty of getting you

26

a room at the Empire Hotel,' he told her. 'No charge, of course.'

'That's very nice of you, Sheriff.' Emily turned to Drifter: 'Were you at the ranch when they – my family – it happened?'

'Yes.'

'Did they suffer?'

'No,' he lied.

Grateful, she hesitated, then forced herself to ask: 'Were they . . . scalped?'

'Miss Emily—'

Emily ignored the sheriff and repeated: 'Were they?'

Drifter nodded, rubbed his nose with his fist, then hoping to ease her pain said: 'But not while they were alive.'

'Praise God for that,' she said, torturing her lower lip.

Sheriff Forbes shot Drifter an angry look, as if telling him he didn't need to go into gory details, and then said: 'Miss Emily, the bodies are at the funeral parlor and Mr Adanski's waitin' for your permission to bury them. We best be goin'.'

Emily continued to look at Drifter, mind churning with questions she didn't dare ask, then she joined the sheriff and they headed into town.

Drifter picked up her bags and followed them.

That afternoon almost the entire town attended the funeral. The tears and heart-wrenching emotions displayed by everyone, even the whores from Lower Front Street, revealed how genuinely sorry they were to lose the Mercers, and Emily would have been forgiven if she'd broken down and wept. Instead, she stoically gritted her way through the minister's graveside prayers and the eulogies delivered by her family's closest friends. Having already cried herself out after receiving Sheriff Forbes's wire, she now seemed more angry than sad; and afterward, when she watched the grave-diggers shoveling dirt on to the coffins and everyone slowly began to disperse, she asked Drifter not to leave, adding: 'I want to talk to you – alone.'

He nodded and stepped back, off to one side, to allow the last of the townspeople to offer Emily their condolences before heading back to town.

Sheriff Forbes was the last to leave. 'You sure you don't want me to walk you to the hotel, Miss Emily?' he asked, hat in hand.

'Yes, thank you.' She waited, motionless, until he'd given Drifter a questioning look and plodded off. Then she thanked Drifter for waiting.

He shrugged and said: 'What did you want to talk to me about?'

'Getting my horses back.'

'You go right to the meat, don't you?'

'If I have to, yes. Well? Will you help me get them back?'

' 'Fraid no one can do that, Emily. By now the Comancheros have driven them across the border and most likely sold the ones they could and eaten the ones they couldn't.'

'I expect to pay you for your services,' she said as if he hadn't spoken. 'Half of what I sell the ranch for. 'Course, you'll have to wait until I do sell it, but that shouldn't take long. Folks were always asking Papa what he wanted for it and—'

'Perhaps you didn't hear me,' Drifter interrupted. 'Even if I did manage to track down *El Carnicero* and his men, which isn't likely since they know the Sierras better than a scorpion, your horses wouldn't be with them. Comancheros are like Apaches, mighty hard on horses,' he added as if to convince her she was wasting her time. 'They ride 'em until they collapse then beat a few more miles out of them before killing and—'

'I'm well aware of how Comancheros treat horses,' Emily said stiffly. 'But not even a Comanchero would kill *or eat* a stallion like Diablo. They'd know he was worth a small fortune and most likely sell him to one of the *rancheros ricos* for breeding purposes.'

Drifter studied her, finding it hard to believe she was serious. 'Let's say you're right. You got any idea how many rich ranchers there are in Sonora and Chihuahua alone, let alone the rest of Mexico?'

'Doesn't matter. We'll just keep looking until we find the right one.'

He almost laughed. ' "We?" You figuring on riding with me?'

'Of course. I've been around horses all my life. Can ride just as well as you or any other man.'

He didn't doubt that. 'Know anything about Comancheros, do you?'

'Only what Pa told me.'

'How about their leader, *El Carnicero*?'

'I know his name means "The Butcher".'

'Do you also know it's not because he owned a butcher's shop?'

Her look of disdain told him she did.

'And you're how old? Twelve? Fourteen, tops?'

'My age is my business,' Emily snapped.

'Not so long as I have to protect you and look after you—'

'Mr Longley,' she said icily, 'no one's asking you to protect me or look after me. I may be young in years, but I'm certainly mature enough to know what I want, what I have to do and to understand the risks facing me.'

'Well, that's good news,' he said. ''Cause that means you're also old enough to understand what I'm going to tell you: there ain't enough money in all of New Mexico to make me chase after a bunch of renegades through mountains full of Mexican *bandidos*. And even if there was, and I was loco enough to accept it, I couldn't be persuaded to take a girl along for the ride, no matter how old she was.'

'Why not?' she demanded. 'What are you afraid of?'

'Everything.'

'Please, be more specific.'

'Specific?' he echoed angrily. 'You're asking me to ride into the devil's lair and now you want specifics?'

'Under the circumstances, I feel I am entitled to them.'

'The hell you are!'

'Mr Longley,' she said firmly. 'You are the last white man to see my family alive. You broke bread with us on many occasions and now everyone is dead but me. I think that could be considered as entitlement.'

Drifter sighed, exasperated. 'OK, then try this for specifics: I don't fancy being roasted upside down over a fire and forced to watch while you're raped and beaten by a bunch of mud-sucking lowlifes hopped up on mescal.'

It was a sobering thought; one that even Emily couldn't ignore.

'Well,' she said, swallowing hard, 'if you won't go after the horses then I'll just have to find someone else who will.' Before he realized, she turned and started down the sloping dirt path to the cemetery gate.

Drifter didn't move until she opened the gate; then he said: 'Why me?'

She paused and looked back at him, the bright afternoon sun forcing her to squint. 'Because Momma trusted you, Mr Longley.'

'Your mother?'

'Yes. Told me so herself. Many times. Said *I* could trust you, too.'

Drifter hesitated, feeling a stab of guilt. 'Then trust me,' he said. 'Do as I tell you and forget about the damn horses.'

'Never.'

'I'd be willin' to help you round up some fresh mustangs. There's plenty in the canyons north of here. If we find the right stallion and breed him to a few select mares, you could start your herd over.'

Emily set her lips stubbornly. 'You don't seem to understand, Mr Longley. I want *my* horses, the horses Pa and my brothers bred so carefully and had such high hopes for – not a bunch of wild, tick-infested broomtails!'

Drifter erupted. 'Dammit, Emily, be reasonable! This isn't a church picnic or a hayride you're goin' on. This is Mexico! You hear me? *Mexico!* A country that's still mostly wild and dangerous, bandits hiding behind every rock, deserts hot enough to fry your brains, and mountains so high they scrape the sun. And if that ain't enough to scare you, consider this: you'll be going up against Comancheros – renegades on a rampage – led by *El Carnicero*, a man who's considered cruel even by Comanchero standards!'

Emily paled and her lower lip trembled, but she managed to hold her chin high. 'Are you finished?' she said when his tirade finally wound down.

'Yeah, I'm finished.'

'Then let me say this, Mr Longley: I appreciate your concern, and I do not think that going to Mexico is anything like a picnic or a hayride. I know it is dangerous, very dangerous, and that I might die there. Inside I am scared, Mr Longley. More scared than I like to admit. But—'

'You're still goin' ahead?'

She said only: 'Would these dangers stop you if they were your horses?'

'Dead in my tracks,' he said.

'Liar,' Emily said politely. She walked out the gate, young, elegant and ladylike, and on into town.

31

CHAPTER SIX

When Drifter entered the livery stable a little later he found Sheriff Forbes playing checkers with the hostler, Lars Gustafson. The two old friends were sitting on overturned crates, huddled over a board resting atop a beer keg, so intent on the game neither looked up as Drifter approached.

'I'll be taking my horse now,' he informed Lars.

The old, gray-bearded Swede waved to show he'd heard and continued concentrating on his next move.

Drifter grabbed the horse blanket hanging over the stall and cautiously sidled alongside the sorrel. Instantly, the horse stepped sideways and tried to crush him against the wall. Half-expecting such a maneuver Drifter kneed the sorrel in the belly, causing it to grunt and move back.

'Try that again, you ugly bastard, and I'll cut off one of your ears.' The sorrel made an ugly snuffling sound but didn't move as Drifter threw the blanket over its back, followed by the saddle.

'He be one mean lug-head, all right,' Gustafson said, without looking up from the board. 'Tried to cow-kick me last night when I brung him his feed.'

'You gonna talk all damned day or make your move?' Sheriff Forbes demanded.

'Why?' said Gustafson. 'You got a hangin' to go to?' He

finally moved, jumping one of the sheriff's checkers in the process. 'Trump that,' he chuckled and spat jaw-juice into a can at his feet.

'How much I owe you?' Drifter said, leading his horse over.

'Pesos or dollars?'

'Dollars.'

'Two'll cover it.'

Drifted handed the hostler two silver dollars, stepped into the saddle, and turned to the sheriff. ' 'Fore I go, there's something you ought to know.'

'I'm listenin'.'

'Emily Mercer: she plans on hiring someone, maybe two or three someones, to help her get her horses back.'

Sheriff Forbes looked up from the board, face creased with concern. 'She actually tell you that, did she?'

Drifter nodded. 'Tried to hire me; said she'd pay me half of what she got from selling the ranch, but I turned her down. She's all set to ride with the men she hires, too, which, knowing the kind of border trash that drifts through here from time to time, could mean she'll end up buried in the desert somewhere. Just thought you'd want to know,' he added, 'you being a close friend of her pa's and all.' He nudged the sorrel forward, ducking his head so his hat wouldn't scrape the top of the door, and then rode off up the street.

Sheriff Forbes sighed wearily and looked across the old tobacco-stained checkerboard at his friend. 'Far as I know, Gus, you ain't never been right 'bout nothin' in your entire life – 'cept once, last year, when you told me to retire.'

'It ain't too late,' Gustafson said. 'Unlike this game, which is good as over for you, you still got some years of livin' left in you.'

CHAPTER SEVEN

Emily stood just inside the batwing doors of the Copper Palace. It was a little after sundown and the large saloon on Lower Front Street, known for its rowdy patrons, easy dancing girls, and the cheap, heavily rouged whores that lived in the rooms upstairs, was filled with miners, cowhands, and border riff-raff, all there to drink, play poker, and raise hell.

For several moments no one noticed the tall teenage girl in her all-black dress, black church-going hat, and button-up boots; then Roy O'Halloran, the head barkeep spotted her and, shocked, immediately stepped out from behind the long curved bar.

'You didn't oughta be in here, Miss Emily,' he said, confronting her. 'This ain't no place for a young lady like you – specially today of all days, with your folks just fresh buried and all.'

'I'm aware of that, Mr O'Halloran, but I have no choice. Time is of the utmost essence. If I am ever to recover my horses I must act immediately.' Lowering her voice, she added confidentially: 'I need to hire one or two men, desert riders, good with a gun and willing to face hardship and danger if necessary, to accompany me into Mexico and track down the Comancheros that raided Pa's ranch. Do you know of any such men you'd recommend for the task?'

O'Halloran looked at her in wide-eyed disbelief. 'Miss Emily,' he said finally, 'I don't mean to be respectful, but you mustn't even consider makin' such a damn fool's journey. Why, you could hire a whole army of men an' it wouldn't do you no good. Not when it comes to trackin' Comancheros. They can disappear faster'n smoke in the wind.'

'I know, but—'

' 'Sides, even if you was able to find 'em, wouldn't matter none. Them horses of yourn are long gone, Miss Emily. Face up to it.'

'Mr O'Halloran—'

'No, no, no more talkin', Miss Emily. Just do yourself and me a favor an' turn around an' go back to Las Cruces. Your folks sacrificed plenty to make sure you got a good an' proper schoolin', so don't you go disappointin' 'em when they ain't around to know better.' Before she could protest he put a large paw on her shoulder, spun her around and guided her to the door.

Outside, alone on the dusk-shadowed boardwalk, Emily tried to think of where to go next to find the kind of men she needed. There were other saloons and cantinas in Santa Rosa, but she knew no one who worked in them and the idea of walking in, cold turkey, and trying to hire strange men to help her retrieve her horses was, well, intimidating to say the least. Still, she had little choice (other than losing her horses and she was too stubborn to accept that); so taking a deep breath to quell her fears, she continued on along Lower Front Street, ready to enter the next saloon she came to.

She hadn't taken more than a few steps when an idea hit her: Sheriff Forbes! Why, he'd know exactly where to find such men, and being a close friend of her pa's she was sure he'd be willing to help her. Spirits lifted, she turned and headed back toward Main Street.

Though evening was closing in, most of the stores were still open and the boardwalk bustled with pedestrians. Many of them recognized her from the funeral. They gave her curious looks, all of them wondering what the hell she was doing alone on the seedy side of town.

Reaching the corner, she turned east and crossed over. Freight wagons, buckboards, riders all passed her, a few too close for comfort, forcing her to jump out of their way. Many of the riders were grubby young cowhands eager to find a bar, card game, or a woman to squeeze for the night. Suddenly, two of them, already drunk enough for her to smell the whiskey on their breath, blocked her path with their horses and made lewd comments to her. She recognized them as the Iverson brothers, two big unruly hands who worked for Stillman J. Stadtlander, a ruthless, powerful rancher whose spread was the largest in the territory.

Emily tried to go around them, but again they walled her in with their lathered cowponies. Trying to hide her alarm, she spoke to the oldest brother, Mace, demanding they get out of her way.

'Now why would we wanna do that, girlie?' he said, leering at her.

' 'Cause if you don't,' she warned, 'I'll tell Sheriff Forbes how you harassed me and he will toss you in jail.'

Mace howled with laughter. 'Hear that, Cody?' he said, grinning at his brother. 'Little Miss Snot-nose, here, is gonna tell the big bad sheriff 'bout us.'

Pretending to be frightened, Cody raised his hands above his head and began to tremble. 'Ooooh, I'm so scared,' he wailed. 'Save me, Mace. Save me! I don't wanna go to no nasty ol' jail!'

Both brothers doubled over with raucous laughter.

Angry at being mocked, Emily tried to force her way between their horses. But the brothers kept a choke-hold on the reins, forcing the horses to stand their ground and keep her walled in with her back against a hitch-rail.

'Let me go!' she hissed at them. 'You hear me? Let me go!'

'Why?' Cody jeered. 'You think 'cause you learned fancy schoolin' you're too good for us?'

'Knowin' your ABCs ain't gonna help you here, missy,' Mace jeered. 'You're on our side of town now an'—'

'Let her go, boys,' a voice said behind them.

The Iversons turned in their saddles and saw Sheriff Forbes standing nearby, thumbs tucked in his gun-belt.

'You heard me,' he said when the brothers didn't move. 'Back up your ponies an' let the lady pass.'

Though he spoke quietly, and made no move toward his six-gun, the cold glint in his hazel eyes warned the Iversons not to buck him.

'We was just funnin' with her,' Mace said, backing up his horse. 'We didn't mean her no harm or nothin'.'

'Glad to hear that,' Sheriff Forbes said. He waited until Emily squeezed out between the horses and joined him before adding: 'Jail's already over-crowded with pig-scum like you.'

The Iversons stiffened at the insult, eyes blazing with anger, but neither reached for his Colt.

'Mr Stadtlander ain't gonna forget the way you treated us,' Mace said, glowering. ' 'Specially come election time.'

'I'll try to remember that,' the sheriff said. 'Now, git!'

The Iverson brothers whirled their mounts around, spurred them into a gallop and rode off.

'You all right, Miss Emily?'

'I'm fine, thank you, Sheriff. And I'm sorry if I've caused any friction between you and Mr Stadtlander.'

'Don't be. I'm hangin' up my star tomorrow, so what Mr Stillman J. Stadtlander – or anyone else for that matter – thinks of me don't mean diddly squat.'

Emily looked shocked. 'Y-you're not going to be sheriff anymore?'

'Nope. Come mornin' I'll be just another ordinary citizen, same as yourself. Why should that bother you?' he asked when he saw her frown. 'By then, you'll be on the noon train for Las Cruces.'

Emily hesitated, eyes cast downward as she toed the dirt with one pointed, button-up shoe. 'I'm not going back to school,' she said finally. 'I'm going after my horses.'

He sighed wearily. 'I heard rumors 'bout that, but figured it was just fools' talk.'

'Well, it isn't,' Emily said. 'In fact I was coming to see you when the Iversons hurrahed me.'

' 'Bout what?'

'See if you knew anyone 'round here – men who can handle a gun, I mean – who'd be willing to help me. I'd pay them, of course, soon as I find a buyer for the ranch. Do you?' she added when the sheriff didn't reply. 'Know any men like that, I mean?'

Sheriff Forbes tugged on his earlobe. 'Only one,' he said.

'Who's that?'

'Me.'

Emily looked at him, astonished. 'Y-you?' Then off his nod: 'You'd help me get my—'

'On one condition,' he cut in.

'What's that?'

'You sign over the deed to your pa's ranch. You're welcome to stay on,' he said as she looked surprised, 'an' to live there long as you like. I wouldn't mind that at all. Or even if you just wanted to come home on school holidays and. . . .' His voice trailed off.

The two stood there, neither seeming to know what to say next, while around them the approaching night was filled with a cacophony of sounds from the various saloons and cantinas.

At last, Sheriff Forbes cleared his throat, politely turned his head and spat into the dirt. 'I know I'm askin' a lot,' he admitted. 'But once I quit bein' sheriff, I'll need a porch to sit an' whittle for the rest of my days. Your pa an' me often talked about me buyin' an acre or two of his on the south fork. Said maybe he an' your brothers might even help me put up a cabin.'

'I'm sure they would have,' Emily said distantly.

'See, I've loved that spread since the first time I saw it when I come out to talk to your pa 'bout rustlers. You weren't big enough to see over a fresh-born calf then, but—'

'I accept,' Emily said.

'You do?'

'I do.'

'You sure?'

'I would not say it if I weren't.'

'I mean I ain't tryin' to railroad you into somethin' you don't want to do, Miss Emily, or might regret later—'

'I know you're not, Sheriff. But as I said, I planned to sell the ranch anyway. So, as long as you're not expecting me to include Diablo or any of the mares we recover in the transaction, you have a deal.' She stuck out her small, firm, gloved hand and looked up at the man looming over her.

'Fair enough,' Sheriff Forbes said, dwarfing her hand in his as they shook. 'I ain't interested in raisin' horses anyways. All I plan to do is eat, sleep and whittle while I watch the goddamn weeds grow.'

CHAPTER EIGHT

The next morning, after a belly-stuffing breakfast of eggs, bacon, sausages, potatoes and flapjacks which, as usual, he charged to his office, Lonnie Forbes handed his star to the surprised mayor and officially resigned as sheriff of Santa Rosa.

He then picked up Emily at the hotel and together they went to the records office in City Hall and transferred the deed for her ranch to his name. As part of the deal, he bought her a horse, a pack mule, and the supplies they would need for their trek to Mexico to recover her horses. He also insisted she change into Levis, boots, a flannel shirt to absorb the sweat, and a wide-brimmed hat to shade her from the intense sun they would encounter for most of the journey. Then, with curious townspeople watching them from the boardwalks, the two rode out of town in the direction of the border.

'Reckon they figure we're loco,' Forbes said as Santa Rosa dissolved into the heatwaves behind them. 'An' maybe we are at that, missy. Loco as a one-eyed coyote chasin' his goddamn tail in the wind.'

'I prefer to think of us as justly determined,' Emily said. 'And by the way, while it's on my mind, Sheriff, I would ask you to please curtail your constant profanity.'

'Be happy to, missy, if'n I knew what the hell curtail meant.'

'Refrain – as in refrain from cussing,' she said. 'Stop using words not fit for church.'

'Well, I'll be sonofa—' Forbes began, then stopped, grinning sheepishly, and spat tobacco juice at a passing rock where it sizzled in the hot morning sun. 'I'll try my damn – honest best, Miss Emily. But if'n I forget and slip up every once in a while, I hope you'll understand that it's my nature to cuss and find it in your heart to forgive me.'

'Of course,' she said. 'Even Pa, who was not one to use profane language in Ma's or my presence, used to slip up occasionally.'

A half-day's ride out of town they stopped at the Buckholtz spread, a small cattle ranch located some fifteen miles southwest of Santa Rosa, to ask the German immigrant owner if he'd seen any sign of hostiles recently. Indeed he had, he told them in his heavily-accented voice. Two days ago, when he'd been looking for strays in the hills, he'd caught a glimpse of Comancheros riding toward the border.

'Did they have extra horses with them?' Emily asked eagerly.

Buckholtz nodded, removed his wire-framed spectacles and wiped the thick lenses on his bleached denim shirt. 'Yah, yah. Many horse,' he said. 'I count, maybe, twenty or twelve.'

'Was Diablo among them?'

'Ziss I do not know, miss. Zere vas much dust and I not zo brave. I hide behind zer rocks until zey pass, I am ashamed to zay.'

'Nothin' to be ashamed of,' Lonnie Forbes said. 'You done right, Mr Buckholtz. If any of 'em had seen you, right about now your scalp would be hangin' from one of their saddles.'

41

'I fear so, yah.'

'And they were definitely headed for Mexico?' Emily put in.

'Yah, yah. Definitely.'

After watering their horses and gulping down a glass of shade-cooled buttermilk, Emily and Forbes thanked Buckholtz and rode off.

The vast sun-scorched scrubland stretched flat as a table before them, flanked on both sides by distant mountains. It was a day's ride to the border and by nightfall they still had more than ten miles to go. Deciding to cross into Mexico in daylight, they made camp up against a pile of rocks which protected them from the cold, swirling winds blowing up from the sierras. Emily watered and fed the animals while Forbes built a fire between their bedrolls, made coffee and skinned and cooked a rabbit he'd shot earlier, all the while trying to ignore the uneasy feeling he had that they were being followed.

It had been nagging at him since they'd left Santa Rosa. He wasn't sure why exactly because he hadn't seen anyone following them or heard anything unusual to make him suspicious. But he felt a 'presence' just the same and occasionally he sneaked a backward glance in hope of glimpsing someone behind them. Each time he'd looked he had made sure that Emily wasn't watching, hoping not to frighten her unnecessarily. Which was why he was caught off-guard when during their meal, she said suddenly:

'Who do you think it is?'

'W-what?'

'The person or persons following us. Who do you think it is?'

'Who said anyone was following us?' he began.

She stopped him. 'Sheriff, I am not a child. So please do not treat me as one. Now, I'll ask you again: who do you think is following us?'

Forbes hunched his massive shoulders in a way that could have meant anything. 'I dunno, Miss Emily. Probably no one.'

'I have the same feeling,' she said as if he hadn't spoken.

'You do?'

She nodded and brushed a piece of rabbit from her lips. 'At first I thought it might be Comancheros. But then I realized that I wasn't being logical. I mean, one man and a woman would never deter *El Carnicero* from attacking us right away.' She paused as she saw his expression and then said: 'Why are you looking at me like that, Sheriff?'

'Like what?'

'Like I'm a complete stranger.'

'In some ways you are, Miss Emily.'

'But you've known me for years, Sheriff.'

'Not up close, like now.' He drained his mug of coffee and threw away the grounds. 'Reckon my problem is, I can't figure you out, Miss Emily. Oh, an' I'd 'preciate it if you'd quit callin' me Sheriff. I ain't a lawman no more and I don't want anyone thinkin' I am – 'specially where we're goin'. The kind of trash that rides the border is always wanted for somethin' and I don't wanna get shot 'cause they think I'm after them.'

'Makes sense,' Emily said. 'You have my word that I shall try my best.' She finished her coffee and yawned before continuing. 'I always thought my pa made the best coffee. But I have to confess, Sher – Mr Forbes, yours is better. She yawned again and gingerly rubbed her backside. 'I'm afraid I have not ridden that often lately, and now I'm suffering for it. Why can't you figure me out?' she asked again. 'Have I changed so much since you last saw me?'

Forbes shrugged and spat into the flickering firelight, making the flames hiss. 'It's kinda hard to explain, Miss Emily. Havin' no young'uns of my own, I got no experience in dealin' with 'em; an' that goes double for a young lady like yourself who's been raised good an' had lots of schoolin'.'

'Yes, I'm sure that it's difficult for you.' She managed a tiny, rare smile. 'I suppose I'm not acting like you or anyone else expected. I could see it in the faces of everyone at the funeral. They kept sneaking looks at me, puzzled looks, as if they were expecting me to break down and cry and have to be coddled and soothed – maybe even put to bed with hot milk.' She paused and looked at Forbes, whose expression indicated that yes, that's exactly what had been expected of her. 'Well,' she continued, 'I have to admit that that's how I felt after reading your wire. I thought my world had ended. I cried and cried and kept asking God to take me too, so I could be with my family again.

'But finally, when I had cried myself out, a strange thing happened: I stopped feeling sorry for myself and became angry – angrier than I'd ever been before. And with the anger came new resolve—'

'New, what?'

'Resolve – determination to get back what was rightfully mine: the horses. Pa paid a lot for Diablo and those mares, and I decided that if I was to ever come face-to-face with him in heaven, I'd feel terribly ashamed if I hadn't done my – my damnedest, as you'd say – to retrieve them.' She finished her coffee and eyed him over the rim of the chipped porcelain mug. 'Do you understand me a little better now, Mr Forbes?'

The former lawman nodded. 'Reckon so.' He studied her for a few moments, mind churning as he absorbed what she'd just said; then he stuck out his huge paw, adding: 'Call me Lonnie.'

Emily shook his hand firmly. 'Only if you'll call me Emily.'

'Deal.'

44

CHAPTER NINE

Drifter added an armful of dry brush to his camp-fire, filled his cup with the last of the coffee, and settled comfortably into his bedroll.

Nearby, the hobbled sorrel snorted and nervously flicked its ears. Drifter pretended not to pay attention to the horse, but under the blanket he grasped the Colt .44 he'd earlier placed beside his leg.

'Hey, the camp!' a voice called out from the darkness.

Drifter relaxed. 'Come on in,' he said. Then, as a tall, slab-shouldered man about his own age, a man leading a magnificent all-black Morgan stallion stepped into the fire-light: 'Figured you'd show up before this.'

'Had to make sure it was you first,' the man said. He had thick, dark hair, a rugged weathered face and deep-set eyes that were an uncanny ice-blue. He wore his cedar-handled Colt .45 in a tied-down holster, gunfighter style, and every movement he made was brief and precise, like a coiled spring ready to snap. 'Then I had to make sure you were alone.'

'Figured that too,' Drifter said. Rubbing his nose with his fist, he added: 'You're gettin' mighty careless for a man chased by a rope.'

'Too much tequila, *amigo*. Livens your soul but deadens your senses. When'd you peg me anyway?'

'Just before sundown.'

'Might've saved me some leftovers.'

'Steak, biscuits an' gravy,' Drifter said, straight-faced. 'My, my, if only you'd gotten here sooner.'

The tall man chuckled. 'I'd settle for coffee.'

'Fresh out.' Throwing aside his blanket, Drifter stood up, holstered his gun and indicated the coffee pot. 'Might be a few grounds left if you ain't particular.'

The man rolled his eyes, muttering 'Judas, Drifter!' and turned back to his horse. Instantly the stallion pricked its ears and danced sideways a step or two. 'Stand still, damn you,' he told it. Approaching the Morgan cautiously, he took a lidded can from his saddle-bag. The horse made no attempt to bite or kick him, something that surprised both men.

'Finally got him quieted down, huh?'

The man, an outlaw named Mesquite Jennings, snorted with disgust. 'Day I believe that is the day the son of a bitch stomps me into my grave.' Looking at the hobbled sorrel, he added: 'See you ain't shot yours yet, neither.'

'Came close a couple of times,' Drifter admitted. 'But then I got to thinking. Having to watch myself around him at all times, keeps me on my toes.'

'Amen,' said Mesquite. 'Knew this Mexican pistol down in Nogales once. Like makin' love to a firecracker with a short fuse. Every time I pissed her off, she'd throw stuff at me – pots'n pans, knives, chairs; whatever was handy. Hell on the nerves, but great for the reflexes.'

Both men laughed.

Drifter waited until the outlaw had poured some ground coffee into the old blackened pot, added water from his canteen and set the pot on the fire. Then he asked: 'Been up visitin' Cally's grave?'

'Uh-huh.'

'How's Mrs Bjorkman?'

'How should I know?'

'Gabe . . . this is me, Quint, you're talking to.'

Mesquite heaved a sigh and said: 'Sorry. Ingrid's fine.'

'And her daughter?'

'Ornery as ever.' He glanced at his horse, muttering: 'I don't know who's a bigger pain in the ass – Raven or Brandy.' At the mention of his name the Morgan stallion snorted and stamped the ground as if resenting the comparison.

Drifter chuckled. ''Bout time you made an honest woman out of that widow.'

'She ain't ready for marriage yet. Told me so herself. Said only time she'd consider gettin' hitched again was when she could look at a man an' not see her husband.'

'Least she's honest.'

'Maybe too honest,' Mesquite grumbled.

They sat beside the crackling fire and drank their coffee in thoughtful silence. Insects whined about their ears. Coyotes yip-yipped to each other in the bone-chilling darkness.

'I saw your poster in the sheriff's office,' Drifter said finally. 'Not much of a likeness.'

'That's how I like it,' Mesquite said. He scratched the week-old stubble darkening his chin. 'Closer to lookin' like you they get, closer to a rope you get. You got paper out on you?' he added.

'None that I know of,' Drifter said.

'Then how come you're high-tailin' it for the border?'

'Long story.'

'We got all night.'

Drifter looked across the fire at the tall handsome outlaw, a man whose real name was Gabriel Moonlight, a man he'd known and trusted for years, and said: 'I aim to pay off an old debt.'

Mesquite chewed on that for a moment before saying:

'Man can always use good company. I'll ride along with you aways – that's if you don't mind ridin' with a horse thief.'

Drifter chuckled. 'Rumor I heard is you won the stallion fair and square in a poker game.'

'You obviously ain't been talkin' to Stillman J. Stadtlander.'

'Wouldn't matter if I had. You're many things, *hombre*, most of them prodding the law, but I'd put my neck in a noose 'fore I'd believe you'd steal another man's horse.'

The outlaw didn't say anything but appreciation showed in his pale-blue eyes. 'I heard about the Mercers,' he said presently. 'We lost a good man.'

'Good woman and two good boys, as well.'

'*Comancheros*!'

Drifter nodded, equally disgusted.

'Wasn't there a daughter, too?'

'Emily.'

'Yeah, that's her. I met her while I was still ramroddin' for Stadtlander. Stubborn little cuss. Looked all prim an' proper, like she wouldn't spit in church, but from what her pa told me, she'd fight you tooth'n nail and didn't have an ounce of quit in her.'

She hasn't changed, Drifter thought.

'Wonder how she'll turn out now she's got no family.'

Drifter stared off into the darkness in the direction of the border. 'She'll be fine,' he said. 'Just fine.'

There was such finality to his words; Mesquite studied him shrewdly.

'You know I ain't one to pry, Quint, but this Emily, she got somethin' to do with the debt you intend to pay?'

'She's got everything to do with it,' Drifter said. 'That's why I'm following her.'

'Emily's up ahead of us?' Mesquite said, surprised.

'With Sheriff Forbes. Don't sweat it,' he said as the outlaw reacted grimly. 'He's not a lawman anymore. Turned in his star this mornin'.'

Mesquite looked shocked. 'Why'd he do that?'

Drifter briefly explained about Emily's quest to recover her stolen horses. He'd been shadowing them since sunup he said, and guessed she'd persuaded Sheriff Forbes to help her track down the Comancheros, offering him enough money to make it worth his while to retire.

'Damn,' Mesquite said. He whistled softly. 'Never thought I'd see the day when that lazy bastard would swap his rockin' chair for a hard saddle.'

'Money talks; conscience walks,' Drifter said. Rising, he threw his coffee dregs into the fire, making the flames sizzle 'Well, reckon I'll turn in. Got a long hard ride tomorrow.'

CHAPTER TEN

Dawn had just broken, turning the sky violet and lemony green, when Emily and her ex-lawman escort crossed the border into Mexico. They crossed where there were no fences, following a narrow, steep-walled ravine that led westward in the direction of Palomas, a small *pueblo* just south of the border that was a known outlaw haven. There was no sign of any hoof-prints, which was disappointing but not surprising since the ravine was called *Canon de los Vientos*, its strong, incessant winds covering everything with shifting sand.

'When we reach Palomas,' Emily said, her voice muffled by the kerchief covering the lower half of her face, 'do you think we should hire one of the locals, someone who is familiar with the area?'

Forbes grunted something that was hidden by the wind. When she asked him to repeat it, he turned to her, squinting against the blowing sand, and through his red kerchief said loudly: 'Well, I can't tell you what to do. But if'n it was up to me, missy, I wouldn't hire no greasers. Couldn't trust 'em. Like as not, they'd rob you blind or lead us in circles hopin' to get more pesos.'

Emily looked surprised. 'Pa hired some Mexicans to help mend our fences after that flash flood two years ago – an old man and his two sons. They were really nice. Pa said they were the hardest workers he'd ever seen. And trustworthy, too.'

'That's 'cause they were in the US, where we got laws. Down here, there ain't no law. Just a bunch of damn *rurales* ridin' around, bullyin' the campesinos and takin' bribes. I know. I chased Mesquite Jennings 'cross the border once, just east of here—'

'Mean the outlaw?'

Forbes nodded. 'His trail went cold but I heard he was holed up in the mountains south of Palomas. Tried to get the *rurales* to help me find him. Fat chance. All they did was laugh an' stick their goddamn – sorry – their dirty paws out for money!'

They rode on, wind gusting in their faces, bombarded by stinging sand and flying objects, broken pieces of mesquite or sagebrush that whipped their cheeks as they blew past.

Finally they were out of the ravine, leaving the wind behind them as they rode across scorched, open scrubland that seemed to stretch forever. There were very few clouds in the brilliant blue sky and as the sun beat down on them, Emily was grateful that the sheriff (she still thought of him as Sheriff Forbes even though she called him Lonnie) had insisted she buy a wide-brimmed hat.

Every mile or so, they reined up to rest the horses and to let Forbes search the sun-baked ground for hoof-prints. There were none. The hours dragged by. Mile after mile of wasteland fell behind them. No permanent trails. No wagon tracks. No hoof-prints. Not even a rattler or scorpion to spit at. As Emily remarked when they stopped to water the horses and the mule and to lunch on beef jerky and hard-tack biscuits: for all the signs of life they'd encountered since sunup, they may as well have been on the moon.

An hour behind them, Drifter and Mesquite Jennings rode at an easy mile-consuming lope. Despite the heat neither the sorrel nor the coal-black Morgan seemed bothered by the pace, making it clear why both riders put up with their unpredictable, irascible horses.

Mid-morning, they reined up beside a low rocky outcrop to give their mounts a blow. It was the first semblance of shade they'd seen since crossing the border. Both men took a swig from their canteens, the water warm and metallic-tasting, then cooled off by wetting their kerchiefs and tying them around their necks.

Feeling refreshed, Drifter filled his cupped hands with water and let the sorrel drink, while Mesquite, wary of being bitten, let the Morgan drink from his old tin coffee mug.

Drifter then climbed to the top of the rocks and scanned the horizon with his field glasses. It took him a moment to get focused, but then the lenses suddenly cleared and he saw them; two tiny wavering riders and a pack mule, blurred by rippling heatwaves, about two miles ahead. 'How much farther to Palomas?' he called down to the outlaw.

'No more'n two hours,' Mesquite said. Then as Drifter slid down and joined him to roll a smoke: 'How long you figurin' on trackin' 'em, Quint?'

'Long as it takes.'

'Past Palomas?'

'Past anywhere.'

'Hair could turn gray by then – if you still got hair, that is, which ain't likely.'

'So be it.'

Mesquite made a face. 'You that anxious to get a head-stone?'

'Hopin' it won't come to that.'

'You – an old, fat, has-been lawman – an' a girl just out of knickers against *El Carnicero* and a bunch of half-breed gunman who qualify as the dregs of humanity? Oh yeah, I sure like those odds.'

'Could always help even out those odds,' Drifter said.

'You askin' for my help?'

'Nope.'

'Sure sounded like you was askin'.'

'Then you got a hearing problem.'

'Don't make no difference anyway.' Mesquite blew a smoke ring and trapped it with his sweat-stained campaign hat. 'There ain't that much gold in all of Mexico.'

'You wouldn't be doing it for gold,' Drifter said.

'There ain't that much tequila, neither.'

'Good. 'Cause I need you sober.'

Mesquite took a final pull on his cigarette then flipped the butt away and squinted at his taciturn companion. 'Not that I give a hoot, *compadre*, but just what is this debt you owe Emily that makes dyin' an option?'

Drifter exhaled the last of the smoke in his lungs and stepped into the saddle without answering. Not until Mesquite was also mounted and had finished cursing the stallion for trying to bite him, did he say: 'It's personal.'

'Be a dirty sonofabitch,' Mesquite said, soft as applesauce. 'You're askin' me to risk my goddamn scalp for a young'un I barely know an' a sheriff I hate an' you won't even tell me why?'

'There's goes that hearin' problem again,' Drifter said.

'OK, so you ain't exactly *askin'* me. But sure as fartin' follows beans, you wouldn't say no if I offered.'

'Sounds about right.'

'Why?'

Drifter shrugged. 'Like you said last night: man can always use good company.'

'It ain't the same thing,' Mesquite grumbled.

'It ain't?'

'Hell, no! You were just ridin' to the border, not attackin' a stronghold held by murderin'—'

'Stronghold?' Drifter interrupted. 'What stronghold?' Then as Mesquite avoided his eyes: 'You know where these bastards are, don't you?'

'I know where they *might* be,' countered Mesquite. 'Least, where they hole up from time to time. But the place is like a goddamn fortress, with lookouts swarmin' around it—'

Drifter cut him off. 'Will you show me?'

'No.'

'Why not?'

' 'Cause, unlike you, I ain't in no rush to die. An' anybody who's loco enough to even try to enter that stronghold uninvited, let alone attack it, is signing his own death warrant.'

'I'm not asking you to attack it, *amigo* – just to lead me there. Soon as you've done that, you're free to ride off.'

'I'm free to ride off now,' Mesquite said. 'I don't have to ride two hundred miles an' risk my neck to prove somethin' I already know.'

'You're right,' Drifter said. 'What's more, what you're saying makes perfect sense. Forget I ever mentioned it.'

'Oh no,' Mesquite said. 'I ain't fallin' for that little game. If you think you can make me feel guilty just 'cause I won't—' He stopped as he realized that Drifter had already ridden off and he was talking to himself.

'Go ahead, take off on your own,' he yelled. 'It don't matter a lick to me. I'm headin' back to my hideout an' there's nothin' you can say to make me change my mind.'

CHAPTER ELEVEN

Puerto Palomas de Villa, known locally as Palomas, was a small, sun-scorched *pueblo* just south of the border. It was nothing more than a scattering of adobe shacks, a few stores, a tiny whitewashed church and several sleazy cantinas that, thanks to no law except for a rare appearance by patrolling *rurales*, catered to a thriving bunch of gringo outlaws and border trash.

Today, as Emily and Forbes rode in, following the rutted, dusty street that snaked through town, they were watched with suspicious interest by the gun-toting riff-raff hanging around outside the various dingy cantinas.

'Promise me somethin',' Forbes said as he ignored the belligerent stares.

'I'll try,' Emily said.

'Let me do all the talkin'.'

'Why?'

'Well . . .' the ex-lawman hesitated, trying to find the words to express himself delicately. 'You got a way of addressin' folks that this trash won't take kindly to.'

She frowned at him. 'Are you saying I'm rude?'

'Borderin' on it, maybe.'

'Why, that's ridiculous. At school the teachers consider me very polite.'

'Maybe that's 'cause you respect your teachers and don't

talk down to 'em,' Forbes said.

Below the wide brim of her hat Emily arched her eyebrows, unable to believe what she was hearing. 'You think I talk *down* to people?'

His silence suggested he did.

'That's absurd. Why would I do that?'

'I dunno. But it's true.'

'Give me an example.'

'Off hand I can't think of one right now.' He removed his hat and with his kerchief wiped the sweatband dry, mopped his face and returned the hat to his head. 'Maybe it ain't what you say exactly, missy, but it's the way you say it. Your attitude.'

'My *attitude*? What attitude?'

He said only: 'Like you figure schoolin' makes you better'n everyone else.'

'Nonsense! I don't think that at all. What's more, Sheriff—'

'Lonnie—'

'I think you're being most unfair in your assessment of me. Perhaps even prejudiced.'

Forbes didn't answer for a few moments, during which time he reined up and dismounted outside a cantina called *El Tecolote*. Then, tying his reins to the hitch-rail, he spat his feelings in the dust and squinted up at Emily: 'Heard a sermon once by Father Quivira. All about people's character and how they should treat their neighbors. Don't 'member most of it but one thing that stuck in my mind was, he said: 'Just 'cause folks use ten-dollar words to describe a ten-cent problem, don't make them ten-dollar people.'

Stung, Emily flushed and momentarily her eyes moistened. Then she regained control of herself, stepped down from her horse and confronted Forbes, wagging her gloved finger in his face. 'That's a very mean thing to say to me,

Sher – Lonnie, and you should be ashamed of yourself for saying it. My pa taught me to treat people the way *I'd* like to be treated, and—'

She broke off, startled, as shots rang out inside the cantina. Moments later, a man holding an ace of spades staggered out and collapsed in the street. Still alive, he tried to get to his knees. It took several attempts but he finally made it and began crawling away. As he did, a second ace of spades fell out of his jacket sleeve. Ignoring it, he crawled on.

Just then two stubbly-bearded, hard-faced gunmen stepped out of the cantina, guns in hand, and shot the crawling man in the back. Four slugs ripped into him, slamming him to the dirt. He grunted, half rolled over, then flopped on his side, dead.

The two gunmen spit on the corpse, holstered their guns and were about to re-enter the cantina when one of them, the younger man, whose gaunt face was disfigured by a knife scar from mouth to cheek, noticed Forbes standing by Emily. He stared at the ex-lawman, trying to place him; then his face split into a wide grin.

'Hells fire,' he said. 'If it ain't our old friend, Sheriff Forbes.'

Immediately his partner turned to Forbes and smiled cruelly. 'I do believe you're right, Zack.' Covering Forbes with his .45, he gave Emily the once-over, adding: 'With his daughter, looks like.'

'I am not his daughter,' Emily began.

Forbes silenced her with a wave of his hand. 'Your quarrel's with me,' he told the gunmen. 'Not the girl.' As he spoke he stepped in front of Emily, his huge hulking frame hiding her from immediate danger.

'That's somethin' you won't have to worry 'bout,' Zack drawled. ' 'Cause you're gonna be lyin' face-down next to that cheater.'

In the next instant three things happened so fast, they seemed to happen simultaneously.

Forbes went for his gun.

Both gunmen started to squeeze their triggers.

Two shots were fired.

Both gunmen staggered back, guns dropping from their limp hands, blood coming from a single hole above each man's heart. Eyes wide with shock, they collapsed and lay still, dead before they hit the ground.

Emily gasped and whirled around to find two dust-caked riders, astride lathered horses, halted a short distance behind her. Each held a smoking Colt.

She recognized one instantly – her folks' friend, the drifter Quint Longley – but it took a moment longer before she remembered the face of the other: Gabriel Moonlight, former foreman at the Stadtlander ranch and now an accused horse thief wanted by the law.

Forbes, who had turned a moment after her, looked surprised as he too recognized Mesquite Jennings.

Both riders holstered their guns, dismounted, and approached Emily and the ex-sheriff.

'You all right?' Drifter asked Emily.

'Y-yes,' she said shakily. Then: 'What're you doing here?'

'Followin' you,' Forbes put in. 'Ain't that right, Drifter?'

'Lucky for you he is,' Mesquite said. 'Or right 'bout now both of you'd be keepin' him company.' He nodded at the corpse in the street.

'I could've handled 'em,' Forbes said, unconvincingly.

'In a hog's ear,' Mesquite snapped. 'You couldn't handle a broom if your office needed sweepin'.'

Stung, the big ex-lawman flushed angrily and started to reach for his gun.

Mesquite grinned, his right hand moving so fast his six-gun seemed to appear magically in his fist.

Forbes, knowing he was beat, froze.

'If you got anythin' worth sayin',' Mesquite said, 'better say it.'

'Leather it!' Drifter stepped between them. 'I told you,' he said to the outlaw. 'He's not sheriff anymore.'

'That don't mean I shouldn't kill him,' Mesquite said, gun trained on Forbes's chest. 'He and his posse have chased me to hell an' back, not to mention the sonofabitch wants to throw a noose on me.'

'That's behind us now,' Forbes said, sounding like he knew he was about to die.

'Behind *you* maybe; not me!'

'You wanna shoot me, go ahead,' Forbes said. 'But not in front of the girl.'

'No one's shooting anybody,' Drifter said firmly. 'You want to ride with me,' he told Mesquite, 'keep that iron leathered.'

Mesquite spoke through clinched teeth. 'You askin' me or tellin' me?'

'Asking,' Drifter said. 'One friend to another.'

Mesquite relaxed, hostility fading, and holstered his gun. Brushing past Forbes, he said, 'I'll settle my beef with you later,' and entered the cantina.

Forbes sagged, relieved. 'Gettin' to be a habit,' he said to Drifter. 'You backin' my fight, I mean.'

'I'm not backing you,' Drifter said. 'This is about Emily. She needs every gun she can get.'

'Mean you're riding with us?' she asked, surprised.

'Looks like,' Drifter said.

'Why? You made it perfectly clear you wouldn't help me in Santa Rosa. What changed your mind?'

Before Drifter could reply, the crowd of border trash that had gathered about the dead bodies now turned ugly. Hands hovering above their six-guns, they started toward him, faces full of menace.

'That's close enough,' Drifter warned. 'Next man takes a

step eats dirt.'

The crowd stopped.

With his left hand Drifter took a Double Eagle from his pocket and tossed it in the dust at their feet. 'Bury 'em,' he said.

'Maybe we should bury you 'longside 'em?' a red-bearded man growled.

'You could do that,' Drifter said calmly. 'Question is, *amigo*, how many of you are willing to be buried with me?' His hand dipped, so quickly that he'd drawn his Colt .44 and had it pressed against the red-bearded man's forehead before anyone realized. 'You first,' he added.

All the fight went out of the red-bearded man. He retreated, hands raised, muttering, 'Not me, mister,' and hurried off.

The rest of the crowd shifted uneasily.

'Any takers?' Drifter asked. Then, when no one answered: 'If it was me, I'd get to burying these men real soon, 'fore they turn ripe in this heat.'

The crowd seemed to agree. Breaking into groups, they picked up the corpses and carried them away.

'I've seen a lot of fast guns in my years,' Forbes said as Drifter holstered his Colt, 'but none faster than you.'

'I know two who are.'

'Name 'em.'

'Mesquite and Latigo Rawlins.'

'The bounty hunter?'

Drifter nodded. 'He's faster than summer lightning.'

'I've heard the name,' Forbes said. 'Lefty, ain't he?'

Drifter nodded. 'But never call him that. He enjoys killing and he'll make it a reason to shoot you.'

'I'll remember that if I ever run into him.'

'You never said why you changed your mind about coming with us,' Emily put in.

Drifter studied her, seemingly on the verge of confiding

60

in her; then changing his mind he indicated the cantina, and said: 'Why don't we all go inside; get some food in our bellies and maybe something cool to drink.'

'Amen to that,' Forbes said. 'C'mon, Miss Emily. Maybe the barkeep knows somethin' about your horses.'

CHAPTER TWELVE

The four of them sat at an old wooden table at the rear of the dim, greasy cantina and chewed down bowls of stringy meat and gravy, black beans and rice. The food was spicy and barely edible, but they were hungry enough to finish everything and then wipe their bowls clean with still-warm tortillas made by a wrinkly old Concho Indian woman they could see sitting on the back step. The three men chased down their meal with beer and shots of tequila; while Emily insisted on making her own lemonade by squeezing a lime into a glass of water.

'Urgh,' Mesquite grimaced. 'How can you drink that?'

'It's really quite refreshing,' Emily said cheerfully. 'And, of course, lime juice is very healthy for you.'

'Healthy?' Forbes said. 'How?'

'Well, for one thing it helps increase the flow of acids in your mouth, which in turn helps digest your food.'

'That's why I suck on a lime after every shot of tequila,' Drifter said, straight-faced. 'To get my acids flowing.'

Mesquite and Forbes chuckled.

Emily continued as if they hadn't spoken. 'Also, when mixed with salt, it's a wonderful purgative.'

'A wonderful *what*?' Mesquite said.

'Purgative,' Drifter said. 'You know: laxative.'

'In other words,' Forbes said, grinning, 'it gives you the trots.'

'Ohhh,' Mesquite said. Then to Emily: 'Why didn't you just say that?'

'I did,' she replied indignantly. 'I can't help it if you're too ignora—' Catching Forbes's warning look, she broke off and then said sweetly: 'Next time I will try to be much clearer, Mr Moonlight. I most definitely will.'

Mesquite glanced about him to see if anyone was eavesdropping before saying quietly: 'Down here, Emily, be better if you called me Mesquite.'

'Very well. And how about you, Mr Longley?' she added to Drifter. 'Do you have another name you'd prefer to be called?'

Drifter shook his head.

Forbes looked sourly at him. 'Dammit, I knew Drifter wasn't your real name.'

'Never said it was. Said it was good as any.'

'You also said that when I found out the reason you weren't usin' your real name, to let you know.'

'Go ahead.'

' 'Cause you're wanted for gunnin' down the Mendosa brothers in Juarez.'

'El Paso,' Drifter corrected. 'We were all in Juarez when they heard I was looking for them, but then they fled back across the border. I followed them and . . . ended up calling them out in front of the Acme Saloon. I would've shot their cousin, Rafael, too, but he ran into the alley beside the saloon and I never did find him.'

'Y-you're a gunfighter?' Emily said, surprised.

'No,' Drifter said. 'Wrangler.'

'First wrangler I ever saw could handle a gun way you do,' Forbes said.

'You hinting at something, *buscadero*?'

'Hell, no,' Forbes said quickly 'Just statin' a fact, *amigo*.

As for you thinkin' I was ever a tough, gun-totin' sheriff – you couldn't be more wrong. Never could jerk a gun fast, even in my prime.'

'Didn't need to,' Mesquite needled. 'You shot all your enemies in the back.'

'That's a dirty lie,' Forbes said angrily. 'I faced everyone I ever arrested.'

'Bury it, you two,' Drifter said. 'Save your quarreling till this is over.'

Mesquite and Forbes glared at each other for another moment, then Mesquite calmed down and told the ex-lawman: 'I knew the Mendosas an' they deserved killin'. Weasels stole some horses Quint was paid to drive to Laredo. Bushwhacked him and left him for dead in the desert.'

'That true?' Forbes asked Drifter.

'Close enough.'

'Just goes to show you,' Forbes said. 'Story I heard was they were in the Acme havin' a drink with John Wesley Hardin an' you shot 'em 'fore they had a chance to slap leather.'

'I've heard that same story,' Drifter said. 'But then a lie always circulates faster than the truth.' Rubbing his nose with his fist, he turned back to Emily. 'C'mon. Let's see if anyone knows anything about where your horses are.'

'That's *my* job,' Forbes said as Drifter and Emily stood up. 'You had your chance to throw in with her an' turned her down.'

'Sit,' Drifter said tersely. Forbes, teeth gritted, sat.

Drifter led Emily toward the bar. Halfway there he stopped and said to her: 'Something you should know: there's a chance the Comancheros are holed up in a strong-hold 'bout three, four days' ride from here. No, let me finish,' he said as she started to talk. 'Mesquite knows where it is and is willing to lead us there—'

'He is? That's wonderful.'

'I said let me finish. This is a long shot at best. Could be neither your horses nor *El Carnicero* and his men are there.'

'But they *could* be, couldn't they?'

'It's possible, yeah. It's also possible that by asking around, we're tipping our hand. Also, might be some of these men at the bar are Comancheros themselves, which means they won't only lie to us, but will try to kill us later.'

'If you're telling me all this hoping to scare me off, you're wasting your time,' Emily said. 'As I told you before, nothing's going to stop from getting my horses back.'

Drifter looked at her with a mixture of admiration and disbelief. 'Just wanted you to know that the odds are stacked against us, is all.'

'That's nothing unusual.'

'Chew it plainer.'

'The odds are always stacked against me.'

'Why do you say that?'

'I'm a girl and this is a man's world,' she said, resigned. 'How much bigger odds could I face?' She walked determinedly to the bar, Drifter hurrying to catch up with her.

The men drinking there, many of them part of the crowd from outside, stared warily at her as she approached, then grudgingly moved aside so she and Drifter could squeeze through.

'We're looking for some horses,' Drifter explained. 'They're wearing a Slash-M brand. Comancheros stole them a few days ago from this girl's ranch outside Santa Rosa—'

'A chestnut stallion with two white stockings and a white blaze between its eyes,' Emily said. 'He's a thoroughbred. You couldn't miss him. Oh, and fifteen mares.'

'We know *El Carnicero* and his men crossed the border

with them,' Drifter continued, 'and we figure they'll try to sell 'em or trade 'em for guns.'

'Been no Comancheros 'round here,' said one man.

'They know better'n to come to Palomas,' said another. 'Ain't that right, boys?' he added to the men along the bar.

As one, they all nodded and grunted in agreement.

'How about you?' Drifter said to the barkeep. 'Seen any Comancheros around? Or any horses matching that description?'

'No, *señor*. I have seen nothing like that.'

'If you have,' added Emily, 'and aren't telling us, you should know I'm offering a reward.'

Ignoring the angry look Drifter shot her, she repeated: '*Estoy ofreciendo una recompensa, señor.*'

Immediately, the barkeep's black eyes narrowed with greed. '*Cuánto es la recompensa, señorita?*'

'Don't say another word,' Drifter told Emily.

'*Cien dólares en oro, señor.*'

The barkeep and the men along the bar all grinned.

'She's lying,' Drifter told them. 'We don't have that much between us in pesos, let alone gold.' Before Emily could protest, he dragged her back to the table and pushed her down into her chair. 'You little fool,' he said angrily. 'You know what you've just done?'

'Maybe gotten my horses back,' she said.

'Made us goddamn targets, you mean! There ain't a man in here – or, soon as word spreads, in any other saloon in Palomas – who wouldn't kill any of us for one gold piece, never mind a hundred.'

'Jesus Joseph, Emily,' Mesquite grumbled. 'You went an' told 'em you had a hundred in gold?'

'Offered it as a reward,' Drifter said. 'Same damn thing.'

Forbes said: 'How the hell were you goin' to pay 'em, girl, if one of 'em had known where your horses were?'

'Gold,' Emily said. 'I have two hundred in twenty dollar

gold pieces hidden in my bedroll.'

The three men could only stare at her in shocked disbelief.

'You lied to me,' Mesquite finally said to Drifter. 'Said this wasn't for gold.'

Drifter ignored him. 'Where'd you get it?' he asked Emily.

'Pa gave it to me.'

'Better think of a better answer than that,' Drifter said. 'I knew your pa. Well. He had more sense than to give you two hundred in gold to spend.'

'It wasn't for spending,' Emily said. 'Least, not for the kind of frivolous spending you're referring to. This was money for schooling. To pay for my books, tuition, uniforms, food, and anything else I needed. Whenever he came to visit me, with or without Momma, he'd give me a twenty dollar gold piece. "Spend it wisely", he'd say. Then he'd say: "Don't tell anyone either, not even your Momma. This is our little secret." '

'But if it was for schooling and things,' Drifter said, 'how come you still got all of it?'

'I don't,' Emily said. 'All in all, Pa gave me fifteen twenty dollar pieces. But I scrimped on everything, bought second-hand text books, washed and sewed my own uniforms, and managed to save ten of them.'

'Be damned,' Mesquite said.

'I'm sorry if I endangered everyone's lives,' she said to Drifter. 'I was just trying to—'

'Get your horses back, yeah I know,' he said, eyeing the men talking animatedly along the bar. 'Let's hope we don't regret it.'

'We will if we don't get out of here,' Forbes said. 'While we still can!' He added to Drifter: 'Since you're runnin' the show now, make your call.'

'I just did,' Drifter said. '*Vámonos!*'

Poised to draw their guns, Drifter, Mesquite and Forbes escorted Emily past the men along the bar, all of whom were looking at her as if she were wolf-bait, out of the cantina.

CHAPTER THIRTEEN

Outside, they quickly untied their horses, swung into the saddles and rode off.

Drifter and Forbes protectively flanked Emily, each man checking his side of the street as they watched for any signs of trouble.

Mesquite brought up the rear. As he rode he pulled his Winchester from its scabbard and half turned in the saddle so that he could see if anyone was pursuing them.

'So far, so good,' he said as they passed the little white-washed church and approached the edge of town.

'Weasels like that don't show their hand right away,' Drifter said. 'They prefer to shoot you in the back or bush-whack you.'

'Gotta get ahead of us to do that,' Forbes reminded him.

'If they did, I know exactly the place they'd jump us,' Mesquite said. 'Blanco Canyon, 'bout three miles south of here. It's a natural maze. One trail in, one trail out. Walled in on both sides by sheer cliffs . . . caves everywhere. Few men with rifles could hold off an army forever. What's more,' he added grimly, 'they don't have to get ahead of us.'

'How d'you mean?'

'Canyon's famous for the *bandidos* living up in the caves. They'll keep us pinned down or try to kill us with a rock-slide. That'll give the bastards in the cantina time catch up to us, trap us in a cross-fire.'

'Why would the bandits want to help those gunmen?' asked Emily.

' 'Cause they're in cahoots,' Mesquite said. 'Don't matter who does the dirty work. They split up whatever gold or possessions they take from the corpses. That way no one goes home hungry.'

'What about the Comancheros? They in on it too?'

'Everybody's in on it, *amigo*. This is *Mexico*!'

'So let's not go through there,' Forbes said.

'Got no choice,' Mesquite said. 'Not if you wanna reach the Comancheros' stronghold. Blanco Canyon sort of funnels into it.'

They rode on, sun burning their backs. Endless, flat, parched scrubland ahead. It was too hot to talk. Almost too hot to breathe. After an hour or so Drifter reined up to spell the animals.

'This stronghold,' he asked Mesquite, 'you ever seen it?'

'Yeah.'

'What's it like?'

Mesquite shrugged and swigged his canteen before answering.

'Mostly, it's a bunch of steep rocky hills, canyons and gorges with lots of hidden trails leading to caves and hide-outs.'

'Anyone hole up there besides Comancheros?'

'Bandits sometimes . . . an' renegade Apaches.'

Drifter eyed him shrewdly. 'How about horse thieves?'

'I hid there when I first came down here, if that's what you're askin',' Mesquite admitted. 'But not for long. A man ridin' solo risks gettin' his throat cut every time he closes his eyes.'

'What about their leader, *El Carnicero*?'

'Met him once.'

'He as mean as they say?'

'Meaner.' He shook his head grimly. 'Mexicans frighten their children into bein' good just by mentionin' his name.' Turning to Emily, he added: 'Be sure to save one round in the chamber . . . 'case you ever get captured.'

'It'll never come to that,' Drifter said. 'I'll make sure of it.' Hooking one leg over his saddle-horn, he stared out across the sun-baked flatland. 'How well you know this area, *compadre*?'

'Well enough. Why?'

'I was thinking – what if we become the hunters instead of the hunted?'

'Meanin'?'

'Between here and Blanco Canyon, is there any place for an ambush?'

'No. It's flatter'n a lake. Unless—' Mesquite frowned, paused, and then said: 'There's a lava bed 'bout a mile ahead.'

'Lava bed?' Emily echoed. 'Mean there was once a volcano around here?'

'Yeah. Way up in the sierras somewhere. Leastwise, that's what this surveyor fella I met once told me. Said millions of years ago a volcano erupted an' spewed out all this molting lava—'

'Molten,' corrected Emily.

Drifter rolled his eyes. 'Go on,' he told Mesquite.

'Says it took a spell to cool off but when it finally did, it stopped flowin' an' hunkered down right where it is now. It ain't perfect for an ambush,' he admitted, 'but it's the only place 'tween here and Blanco that offers any real cover.'

'Lead the way,' Drifter told him.

The noon sun hammered down on the vast bed of black, cinder-like rocks and knobby ridges of lava strewn across the scrubland that led to Blanco Canyon. Here, the heat was even more intense and little or no plant life existed in the arid, cracked earth. There was no trail either. The closest thing to one was an old dry river-bed that ran curving through the middle of the lava bed. Drifter, with Emily beside him, took cover on one side while Mesquite and Forbes positioned themselves on the other.

'Hope them sonsofabitches don't wait too long to come after us,' Forbes grumbled, 'else we're gonna fry up crispier than bacon.'

Mesquite grinned at the ageing ex-lawman. 'What's the matter, old man? Wishin' now you'd hung on to your cushy job?'

'Where the hell would you sooner be, sonny,' Forbes snapped. 'Here or rockin' in the shade outside my office?'

Before Mesquite could answer, he saw several riders appearing on the horizon. Due to the heatwaves, they seemed to be floating rather than riding, and he rubbed his eyes before looking again to make sure he wasn't imagining things. He wasn't. 'Riders comin',' he called across to Drifter.

'How many?'

' 'Round a dozen, looks like.'

Drifter raised his field glasses to his eyes, screwed the lenses around and suddenly a group of riders jumped into vision. 'Ten,' he said, counting. 'All armed to the eyeballs.'

Beside him Emily, clutching the extra Colt he'd loaned her, asked: 'Is it the gunmen from the cantina?'

'That'd be my guess.'

'Oh dear God,' she said, eyes moistening. 'This is all my fault. I feel terrible.'

'Forget it,' Drifter said. 'If they've got a deal with the *bandidos* in Blanco Canyon, like Mesquite says, they would've come after us anyway.'

'I'll never disobey you again,' she promised. 'No matter what. I'll do exactly as you say.'

'I hope you mean that.'

'I do. I give you my word.'

'Good,' Drifter said. 'Then obey me now. Go and stay with the horses; make sure the shooting doesn't spook them.'

'But I can shoot straight,' Emily protested. 'You might need me.'

'So, your word means nothing?'

'No . . . I mean yes, yes, it does, but I caused this and I want to help you.'

'You want to help me, do like I say and take care of the horses. Do it,' he said as she hesitated. 'There's going to be a lot of killing soon, ugly killing – men and horses shot and dying – and I don't want you to be a part of it.'

'You're not my father,' she said stubbornly. 'You have no right to tell me what to do.'

For a moment Drifter studied the earnest, farm-fresh, dark-eyed face looking up at him. Inside he felt emotions tugging him in all directions. Finally, he said: 'If I were your father I'd tell you this: never give your word unless you mean to keep it. A person's word says everything about them. It's like a blueprint of their life; their character. It tells you if you can trust them or not.' He cupped his hands about her face, adding gently: 'Can I trust you, Emily?'

'Yes,' she said after a long pause.

'Good.' He turned his back on her, raised his glasses to his eyes and studied the oncoming gunmen.

Emily didn't move. She hated to leave but something in his tone, his eyes, told her to obey him and, grudgingly, she hurried along the wash to a long low ridge of lava rock where earlier they had left the hobbled horses.

Relieved, Drifter made sure she was safe then faced front and watched the riders drawing closer.

'Hey, *Jefe*!' Mesquite yelled from the other side of the arroyo. 'How you wanna do this? Hit 'em straight on or wait for 'em to pass – what?'

73

'Let the first two or three pass, then open up,' Drifter said. 'Cause more confusion that way.'

It took the riders about ten minutes to reach the lava bed. They were in no hurry and some of them were confident enough to pass a bottle back and forth.

As they drew close the sights of three unseen Winchesters were trained on them. And once the three men up front had ridden past the ambushers, those rifles opened fire into the seven riders following.

Immediately two riders toppled from their saddles, dead before they hit the dirt. A third slumped over but briefly managed to hang on to his horse's neck until he suddenly pitched forward, arms akimbo, and his wounded horse stumbled and went down.

Instant confusion.

The alarmed riders following tried to rein up. But the momentum of their horses couldn't be stopped and they plowed into their fallen comrades, their own mounts rearing up in panic as more lead was pumped into them. The chaos was increased as the three front riders whirled around and came galloping back, guns firing.

Drifter, Mesquite and Forbes kept their heads down, firing until their rifles grew hot. Round after round poured into the startled gunmen, knocking two more of them from their horses, causing even more confusion and panic.

Finally, shooting wildly at an enemy they couldn't see, the remaining five gunmen whirled their mounts around and spurred them back toward town.

Drifter sighted quickly and fired, knocking another rider out of the saddle. Across the wash Mesquite and Forbes gunned down two more men.

'Let 'em go!' Drifter yelled, referring to the last two gunmen. 'It'll be a warning to anyone else who tries to follow us.'

It was over then. The silence following the shooting seemed to be even more deafening than the gunfire.

Drifter, Mesquite and Forbes warily approached the bodies. The men who weren't dead were dying. Their horses were scattered about the dry river-bed. Drifter killed one horse that was down and thrashing helplessly; Mesquite shot another. The shooting frightened the other horses, sending them loping back toward town.

Forbes hunkered down beside a dying gunman, unscrewed the cap of his canteen, and placed it to the man's lips. He died before he could drink. Forbes stood up, took a swig himself, and grimly surveyed the slaughter.

'Hell of a thing to kill a man,' he said to no one in particular. 'Even when he deserves it.'

Drifter and Mesquite ignored him.

'You figure they heard the shooting?' Drifter asked the outlaw, who was gazing toward the distant outline of Blanco Canyon.

'Depends on the wind . . .' Mesquite sucked his finger and held it up. 'Doubt it. It's blowin' toward us.'

Drifter nodded his approval and signaled to Emily, who was peering around the lava ridge. 'It's over,' he told her. 'Bring the horses.'

Forbes came up and indicated the corpses. 'We gonna bury 'em or leave 'em to the buzzards?'

'Let 'em rot,' Drifter said coldly. 'But collect all the ammo you can. We might need it later.'

CHAPTER FOURTEEN

With their horses and the mule watered and well rested, the four of them rode toward Blanco Canyon. They followed the same wash that once, millions of years ago, had been a deep, fast-moving river and was responsible for carving out the present-day shape of the canyon. It led them directly to the entrance – two steep, towering pinkish-white cliffs that formed a giant V on either side of the narrow wash.

When they were within a hundred yards of it, Drifter reined up his horse. Waiting for the others to do the same, he then asked Mesquite how far it was to the other end of the canyon.

'A mile or so,' the outlaw said, adding wryly, 'sure seems a hell of a lot longer when you're gettin' shot at from all angles.'

Drifter said: 'If my plan works, maybe we can avoid that.'

The others looked at him curiously.

'Plan?' Emily said. 'What plan?'

'A good magician,' Drifter said with a faint smile, 'never reveals his secrets.'

The lookout came scrambling down from a ridge overlooking the canyon and ran to a campsite. Protected on all sides by huge boulders, it sloped up to the entrance to a large cave. Outside the cave a dozen bandits sat eating around a small fire. Unwashed and ill-clothed, they wore high-crowned sombreros and ammunition belts crisscrossed over their chests and shoulders. All carried old single-shot US military-issue pistols and beside each man lay a Springfield rifle, trapdoor single shot model that had been stolen from an army supply train heading for Fort Bliss, Texas.

The leader, Adolfito Baca, a slender man of forty with lank black hair, fierce dark eyes, and a Zapata mustache, folded his tortilla and dipped it into a pot of black beans cooking over the fire. He then stuffed it in his mouth, bean juice running down his chin.

The lookout, unwilling to disturb his leader while he was eating, stood there, meek and silent, until Baca finally looked up.

'*Qué es, Paco? Algien viene?*'

'A man and a girl, *Jefe*, with a pack horse.'

'*Gringos?*'

'Sí, Jefe.'

'Who else?'

'No one, *Jefe.*'

'Just the two?'

'*Sí, Jefe. No más.*'

'You are sure of this?'

'*Sí, Jefe.* I wait and wait . . . but no one come.'

Baca frowned, puzzled, and spoke to the other bandits. 'These must be very poor gringos,' he said, 'or else they would have been robbed and killed in Palomas.' His men nodded in agreement.

'Unless,' one of the bandits said, 'the gringos kept to the outskirts and were not seen.' Again, the other bandits nodded in agreement.

'We should kill them anyway,' an older bandit said. 'Three horses are better than no horses.'

Baca nodded. He sucked his fingers clean and wiped them on his white cotton pants. Then rising, he collected his rifle and ordered the lookout to show them where the *gringos* were.

As they followed the dusty, winding trail through Blanco Canyon, Emily and Forbes tried to appear at ease, but the sweat running down their faces was not all due to the broiling heat. They rode their horses at an agonizingly slow pace, eyes fixed straight ahead, feigning drowsiness as if they had all day to pass through the canyon. But inwardly every part of their body was tensed in expectation of shots ringing out. Slowly the trail unwound ahead of their plodding horses; bleached white limestone cliffs loomed up on both sides of them, their ancient chiseled walls so steep in places the tops seemed to be holding up the sun.

'Under different circumstances,' Emily said, taking a sip from her canteen, 'this would be a beautiful place.'

'Under different circumstances,' Forbes grumbled, 'we wouldn't *be* here.'

'Mean if I hadn't been so mule-head stubborn about getting my horses back?' When Forbes grunted, but didn't answer, she said: 'I'm not sorry for coming, you know, not even if I get killed.'

'Never figured you would be.'

'As I told you in Santa Rosa, those horses meant everything to Pa and—'

She broke off, alarmed by a sudden rumbling overhead. Looking up they saw boulders, rocks and dirt raining down on them.

'Get back!' Forbes yelled. 'Turn around! Go! Go!' Even as he spoke he grabbed her reins and, whirling his horse around, pulled her mount along with him. Both horses reared, almost unseating their riders, and then, terrified by the onrushing rockslide, bolted back the way they'd come.

None of the falling rocks touched them, but within moments the trail was sealed off behind them. They raced back around a curve and had only gone a short distance, when a second rockslide came crashing down – this one blocking the trail in front of them.

They were trapped.

Both riders reined up. As their horses slithered to a stop, rifle shots came from high up in the cliffs and bullets ricocheted off the canyon walls.

'Take cover!' Forbes shouted. 'Hurry!'

Emily obeyed, jumping from her saddle and diving behind the nearest fallen rocks. Forbes dismounted, grabbed his Winchester from its scabbard and lumbered after her.

'You OK, missy?' he asked as he hunkered down beside her.

'Uh-huh. You?'

His reply was hidden by another burst of rifle fire overhead. They ducked their heads as bullets chipped away at the rocks all around them. Pinned down, they remained huddled together for several minutes, bullets whining about their ears.

'Can you see 'em?' Forbes asked as a lull in the shooting allowed Emily to peek over the rocks.

She nodded, her gaze traveling over the rocks about halfway up the cliff facing them. 'One . . . two . . . thre – no, four on this side and. . . .' She glanced behind them, 'two . . . three . . . maybe five or six up there.'

'Got us pinned down, the bastards.'

More gunfire. More bullets ricocheting around them.

Forbes sighed, troubled, and looked at Emily. 'Galls me to just sit here and let 'em take potshots at us.'

'It's what we agreed on,' Emily reminded, him.

Not listening, Forbes grimly eyed the *bandidos*. 'Just say the word, Miss Emily. I could nail one or two of the sonsofbitch – I mean, what the hell, you're payin' me to protect you an' I can't do that if I give up my—'

'It's all right,' she broke in. 'We said we'd follow Mr Longley's plan, and by golly, that's what we're going to do.'

The big ex-lawman nodded reluctantly, 'OK, missy. Just wanted to make sure. Better give me your hanky then, so they can see we're surrendin'.'

CHAPTER FIFTEEN

Led by their leader, Baca, the *bandidos* on the east cliff cautiously descended from their hiding places, using a narrow, twisting, treacherously steep path that led to the floor of the canyon. Meanwhile, their *compadres* on the west cliff remained in their positions, rifles trained on the two *gringos* below.

Emily and Forbes watched them coming. Forbes held his rifle in the air, waving Emily's white handkerchief that was tied to the muzzle. At his feet lay his six-gun, thrown there a few minutes ago when they had surrendered.

Finally Baca stopped in front of Emily and with mock politeness, removed his sombrero. '*Buenas tardes, señorita*. It is a fine day for a robbery, *sí*?'

'Depends on who's gettin' robbed,' Forbes said.

'You're wasting your time,' Emily said. 'We have nothing to steal.'

Baca repeated her remark in Spanish to his men, who all laughed.

'I am sorry, *señorita*. But as you see, my men, they do not believe you.'

'Then search us,' she said. 'See for yourselves.'

Baca barked an order and three of the men hurried forward, one searching Emily, another Forbes, a third the pack mule. Using his machete, the latter cut the rope holding the tarp over the supplies. Tossing the tarp aside, he quickly hacked open each bundle, revealing bedrolls, cooking utensils, clothing and canned food.

'*Nada, Jefe,*' he said to Baca.

The man searching Forbes's pockets found a few US bills and a handful of coins, all of which he handed to Baca.

'*Nada, Jefe,*' the man searching Emily said.

'See, I told you,' she said to Baca. 'I have nothing. Everything I had of value – my mother's emerald brooch, a diamond ring, ten gold pieces, a silver hand mirror – was stolen from me by those despicable thieves in Palomas.'

'They would've stolen my money too,' put in Forbes, 'but I had it hidden in my boots.'

Baca frowned, unconvinced. 'I do not believe you. Either of you. I know these men you speak of. They would not have just stolen your money and jewelry; they would've had taken your horses, too, and then killed you.'

'They intended to,' Emily said. 'But I begged one of them, a big man with a gray beard, not to kill me. I told him Comancheros had just killed my folks, and that this man, my uncle, was taking me to Mexico City so I could live with his sister.' As she spoke, trying her best to hold Baca's attention, Emily saw Drifter and Mesquite climbing over the rocks behind the *bandidos*.

She immediately began to fake tears, begging: '*Por favor, señor . . . no nos maten. No nos maten. . . .*' When Baca didn't respond but continued to glare at her, she added: 'Surely you must have daughters of your own, daughters whom you love and would not want killed—'

'*Silencio!*' Baca raised his hand to quiet her. 'You are wrong, *señorita*. I have no daughters; only sons, and two of those were killed by *gringos . . .* miners searching for gold in Canyon del Oro—' He broke off as one of the lookouts above them spotted two men climbing over the rock barricade behind Baca, and opened fire.

Bullets kicked up sand at Drifter's feet.

Instantly, Mesquite spun around and snapped off a shot at the lookout. He dropped his rifle and his body came flopping down from above.

At once Baca and his men whirled, saw Drifter and Mesquite running toward them, and began firing.

Drifter and Mesquite hit the dirt and fired from their stomachs.

Two of Baca's men crumpled and fell. Dead.

Simultaneously, Forbes lowered his rifle and quickly pumped several rounds into the rest of Baca's men. They dropped before they could pull their triggers, leaving Baca the only man standing before Emily.

It was over in seconds.

Jumping up, Drifter jammed his rifle into Baca's back. 'Drop it! Now!' Then as Baca hesitated: 'Do as I say! *Pronto*! Or I'll blow you wide open.'

With Baca as a hostage, Drifter, Emily, Mesquite and Forbes watched as the remaining *bandidos* cleared away the rocks blocking the canyon exit.

When finally the opening was big enough for them to ride through, Drifter warned the *bandidos* not to pursue them and then made Baca walk ahead of them until they were out of Blanco Canyon.

'You have won this time, *gringo*,' Baca told Drifter. 'But one day you will have to come back this way . . . and I shall be waiting for you.'

'Thanks for warnin' us,' Mesquite said and shot him.

There was a stunned silence.

'H-how could you do that?' Emily scolded. 'He was unarmed.'

Mesquite pinned her with a cold, pale-blue stare. '. . . "For all they that take the sword shall perish with the sword." Gospel of Matthew. Verse 26.25.' He rode off.

Taken aback Emily looked questioningly at Drifter, who shrugged.

'That's Gabe for you. His pa was a circuit preacher in the gold camps of California. The boy learned real early the meaning of kill or be killed.'

CHAPTER SIXTEEN

They rode at an easy lope until sunset and then made camp in a shallow arroyo near some low brown hills. They were now almost one hundred miles from the border and, according to Mesquite, the only person in the group who had been this deep into Mexico before, the hills were a prelude to the mighty Sierra Madre Occidental at the foot of which was the Comancheros' stronghold.

Emily, who seemed to have forgiven Mesquite for shooting an unarmed man, was suffering from saddle sores. She didn't complain about them, and no one would have known there was anything wrong if Drifter hadn't noticed her wincing each time she took a step.

'It's nothing,' she said when he asked why she was limping. 'Just a few blisters. I haven't ridden since I went to school, so it's to be expected.'

'I got something that'll help you,' Mesquite said. Going to his saddle-bags he took out a small, round, flat tin marked: A. Thomas & Son – Grape Brand Chewing Tobacco.

'You want her to start chawin'?' Forbes said incredulously.

Mesquite ignored the ex-lawman and opened the tin to

show it contained a dark, foul-smelling grease. 'A Mescalero shaman give me this,' he explained to Emily.

She took a sniff and grimaced. 'Urgh! Thank you, but I think I'll be all right.'

'Do as I say an' rub it on the blisters,' the outlaw insisted. 'They'll be healed tomorrow.' Seeing the looks of doubt on the faces of his companions, he added: 'I ain't foolin'; it's mighty potent stuff. Heals sores and wounds like it's a miracle.'

'Mean you've actually tried it?' Emily said.

Mesquite nodded. 'More'n once. Never failed.'

When Emily still looked dubious, Drifter said to Mesquite: 'Tell her about Lolotea.'

Mesquite shook his head.

'What's Lolotea mean?' Emily asked, curious. 'Please tell me,' she said when he didn't answer. 'I'd really like to know.'

Mesquite took a deep breath as if remembering a painful memory, and stared into the dancing firelight. 'A while back, I got shot an' was close to dyin'. This widow and her daughter, Raven, found me in the desert an' took me back to their spread. Raven fetched a shaman, Almighty Sky, from the reservation. 'Cause he was a friend of the widow's husband, he brought this sacred healer with him. It was the first time she'd been allowed to leave the reservation. Her name was Lolotea, which in Apache means Gift from God, which she surely was. She was about your age, Emily, only blind, real pretty an' had long prematurely white hair. She stayed all night with me in the Bjorkman barn, chanting and praying to the Spirit gods. I was unconscious, so I don't remember nothin' that went on. But accordin' to Ingrid, the widow, the next mornin' I came back from the dead and started to mend.'

'And Lolotea gave you this medicine?' Emily said.

'Uh-huh. All her power was in her hands an' in her faith.

Wasn't until the Apaches were leavin' that Almighty Sky give me the medicine, sayin' I was to rub it on the wound until it disappeared – which I did. The medicine was in a little clay pot then. I kept it with me for a spell, then the pot got broken so I transferred it to this tin. Been carryin' it around ever since.'

Emily considered for a moment and then smiled. 'What a remarkable story,' she said.

'Or one hellacious tall tale,' muttered Forbes.

Emily ignored him. 'I wish I could meet Lolotea, she sounds wonderful.'

'She was,' Mesquite said, adding sadly: 'She's dead now. Reckon the Good Lord figured she was too special to waste on us ordinary folks.'

There was a strange silence around the fire as everyone seemed lost in their own thoughts.

Then Emily took the little tin from Mesquite, saying: 'I've changed my mind. Think I'll do as you suggest and rub it on my blisters. Goodnight all.' Rising, she walked off behind some rocks.

'That yarn you just spun,' Forbes asked Mesquite, 'it got any truth in it or did you just trump up the whole thing so Emily would use the grease?'

'What do you think?' Mesquite said. He winked at Drifter then spread his bedroll, climbed under the blanket and was asleep almost immediately.

'Sonofabuck is lyin' through his teeth,' Forbes said. 'I know he is.'

Drifter shrugged. He'd often heard Apaches – especially Mescaleros – talking about Lolotea in reverent, spiritual terms, but had always thought she was merely part of Apache folklore. Now he wasn't so sure.

'Get some shuteye,' he told Forbes. 'I'll take the first watch.'

*

It may have had something to do with the grease, then again maybe not, but the fact was that in the morning when Emily joined Drifter, Forbes and Mesquite at the breakfast fire, she was smiling.

'All healed,' she announced. Then handing Mesquite the tin: 'You're right; it's like a miracle. I can't thank you enough.'

'It's the Apaches you should be thankin',' Mesquite said. 'They're the ones worked the miracle.'

Forbes spat his disgust into the fire. 'All this goddamn nonsense 'bout Apaches an' miracles is makin' me sick,' he grumbled. 'If Injuns can work miracles, how come they can't heal 'emselves an' are starvin' to death on reservations? Huh? An' if they're so damn holy why'd they use to butcher an' scalp folks, innocent folks, includin' women and young'uns? Huh? Maybe one of you Injun lovers can explain that to me!' Scraping the remains of his beans and bacon into the fire, he stomped over to his horse, rinsed off the plate with water from his canteen and tucked it into his saddle-bag.

'What's eatin' him?' Mesquite said.

'Utes killed his kid brother,' Emily said.

Mesquite frowned, surprised. 'I never knew that. Did you know that?' he asked Drifter.

'Uh-uh. How'd you find out?' Drifter said to Emily.

'Pa told me. Said Lonnie found what was left of his brother staked out over an ant hill. He's never gotten over it. Hated all Indians ever since.'

'Understandable,' Drifter said. 'Maybe not reasonable, but definitely understandable.'

'It's how I feel about the Comancheros,' Emily said. 'I never ever thought I could wish anybody any harm – I don't even like to step on bugs. But every night now I go to sleep wishing I could kill them all.'

'Don't worry. You'll get your chance,' Mesquite said

grimly. 'Me'n Quint are gonna see to it.'

Drifter looked at him, puzzled. Later, when the two of them were tying their bedrolls behind their saddles, he said quietly: 'When'd you change your mind, Gabe?'

' 'Bout what?'

'From guiding us to fighting with us?'

Mesquite chuckled. 'My mind was made up all along, compadre. I just wanted to jerk your tail for a spell 'fore I told you. By the way,' he said before Drifter could respond, 'few miles south of here we're gonna be makin' a slight detour.'

'What for?'

'To pick up a little surprise for our Comanche-lovin' friends.'

And that's all he would say about it.

CHAPTER SEVENTEEN

The cabin was at the far end of a broad valley, built atop a steep rise that afforded panoramic views of the surrounding mountains from its only door and rear window. Nearby was a small barn and behind the barn were two rocky outcrops that stood like sentries guarding a dry stream-bed that, during the rainy season, was fed by water coming down from the mountains.

The four of them entered from the northeast. Though it was still early morning, already the heat was unbearable, and the weary riders kept their sweat-caked horses at a slow steady walk. The Morgan appeared to be less tired than the other horses, and as they got closer to the cabin the all-black stallion pricked its ears and quickened its gait as if eager to reach the barn.

'Looks like he knows where he's going,' Emily said.

'He ought to,' Mesquite replied. 'It's been his home for quite a spell.'

'*This* is where you hole up?' Forbes exclaimed. He looked about him at the parched, desolate scrubland, adding: 'In this godforsaken place? Jesus-Mary-Joseph! No wonder no lawman's ever tracked you down.'

'Wouldn't have done 'em no good even if they had,' Mesquite said. 'I would've picked 'em off like ducks on a pond 'fore they got halfway way 'cross the valley—' He stopped talking as the stallion suddenly bucked, almost throwing him off. 'Damn you!' he cursed, swiping the Morgan's head with his hat. 'Quit that or I'll—' Again he stopped as this time the stallion reached back to bite his leg. Mesquite jerked his boot out of the stirrup just in time to avoid the snapping teeth. 'Sonofabitch, Brandy, I swear I'm gonna put lead right 'tween your ugly ears one day!'

'Pa had a horse like that,' Emily said as they rode on. 'A roan mare named Tippy. Used to kick and try to bite him every chance she got. Momma begged him to get rid of her 'fore he lost a finger or something. But he never did. Wouldn't say why but I think deep down it was because he kind of respected her and . . . and. . . .' Emily paused, voice choked with emotion, and turned her head away so none of the men would see she was crying.

When they finally reached the cabin, they were limp and exhausted.

'I thought it was hot in New Mexico,' Emily said as she fanned herself with her hat. 'But this is like being in a furnace.'

'It ain't gonna get any cooler where we're goin',' Mesquite warned. 'So if you wanna call it quits—'

'I don't!' Emily snapped, cutting him off. 'I've no intention of ever quitting! What's more, I'd appreciate it if you would not bring that subject up again.'

' 'Scuse me, ma'am,' Mesquite humbly tipped his hat and reining up, dropped back beside Drifter and Forbes. 'Well, one thing's for damn sure,' he said, chuckling, 'all that schoolin' sure ain't dampened none of her feistiness.'

'Amen,' said Forbes.

'Funny thing is,' Mesquite added. 'I don't recall her pa bein' that salty. Fact is, any time we talked he seemed kind of easy goin' and mellow.'

'What do you expect?' Drifter snapped. 'She's only four-

teen and just buried her whole goddamn family!'
Dismounting, he turned his back on the outlaw and began
loosening the cinch straps.

Mesquite rolled his eyes at Forbes. 'Is it me, or is everyone on the prod today?'

'It's this damn heat,' the ex-sheriff said. 'Dries up the
sweetness in a man's soul quicker'n grease in a fryin' pan.'

Deciding to remain there until late afternoon when the sun
cooled off a little, they unsaddled the horses, watered them
from the canteens, and then hobbled them in the shade
behind the barn.

It was a few degrees cooler inside the one-room cabin,
and keeping the door propped open with the only existing
chair they spread their bedrolls on the dirt floor and
flopped down to take a nap.

Mesquite woke first and went outside for a smoke. Drifter
joined him moments later and after lighting up, said:
'Before the others wake up, what's this surprise you mentioned?'

Motioning for Drifter to follow, the tall outlaw led him
into the barn. It too, had a dirt floor and a makeshift
hayrack above a single horse stall. A ladder leaned against
the rack. Mesquite started up it, saying: 'Give me a hand.'

Drifter climbed up the ladder after him.

Crouching down to avoid hitting his head on the roof
beams, Mesquite moved across the loose hay to a wooden
box in the corner. Waiting for Drifter to join him, he
explained that the box contained dynamite. 'Don't worry,'
he added as Drifter immediately recoiled. 'It's only been
here for a month or so, so it won't have sweated too much.'

'If you say so,' Drifter said uncertainly. He watched
tensely as Mesquite gently lifted the lid to expose some
twenty sticks of dynamite buried in loose straw. Mesquite
carefully examined each one. A few, near the bottom, had

'weeped' a little and he cautiously wiped the nitroglycerin crystals away, until the bright red wrapping paper was dry.

Drifter unconsciously held his breath until Mesquite was finished, then exhaled loudly. The outlaw grinned at him. But there was a look in his eyes that told Drifter he knew how dangerous the last minute or so had been.

'What the hell you doing with this anyway?' Drifter asked as Mesquite gently repacked the dynamite. 'You planning on becoming a prospector?'

'Not in this lifetime,' Mesquite said. 'Too much work for too little return. No,' he continued, 'I kind of got stuck with it. I was up in Silver City one night an' this miner I knew needed money to pay off a poker debt. I told him I wasn't no bank, but when he swore he'd pay me back double, I agreed. It was only supposed to be for a few days, a week at most, 'cause by then he figured to have dug triple what he owed me out of his mine.'

'So what happened?'

'Got bushwhacked by claim-jumpers.'

'Jesus. So why didn't you sell it to another miner or a mining company, plenty of both in Silver City.'

'Plenty of law, too. An' when you're an accused horse-thief with a price on his head, it ain't healthy to stay in one place too long. Anyway,' he added as he reburied the final stick, 'turns out, it's lucky for us the poor bastard got killed. Otherwise, we wouldn't have this dynamite. I mean, I ain't no military genius when it comes to attackin' strongholds, but if we can find a way to put this boom-boom to good use, suddenly the chances of us gettin' those horses from the Comancheros don't seem so impossible.'

Drifter said: 'Where're the caps or fuses?'

'Don't have none,' Mesquite replied. 'Like I said, I didn't figure on holdin' on to the dynamite that long.'

Drifter chewed his lip thoughtfully. 'That may be a problem, *amigo*.'

'Not for a good shot. As a young'un, when I was travelin' the gold camps with Pa, miners used to use dynamite for target practice. You hit it solid an' it explodes just fine.'

'Maybe so. But first we have to sneak past those lookouts you mentioned then get into the stronghold and plant the sticks in strategic positions, which won't be easy. And if one of us is spotted, even if we aren't shot or captured, it kills any chance we have of surprising them. What we really need,' Drifter added, 'is a way of launching the sticks into the stronghold then shooting them after they land.'

Mesquite thought a moment. 'I got an idea,' he said. Going to a corner of the barn, he grabbed something leaned against the wall there, and returned with an unstrung bow and a quiver of arrows.

'Where'd you get those?'

'I made 'em.'

'You made them?'

'Made 'em.'

'Didn't know you were ever that friendly with the Apaches.'

' 'Paches didn't teach me to make this bow; the Tarahumara did.'

'Tarahumara? Never heard of them.'

'They don't want you to hear of 'em. Or see 'em. They're reclusive. Live high in the Barranca del Cobre. Call themselves the Raramuri – the Runners – 'cause they can run all day without gettin' tired. Fact is it's the way they hunt, by runnin' down a deer until it's exhausted, then slittin' its throat.'

'So why do they need bows and arrows?'

'Defense mainly – against prospectors lookin' for gold in the Sierras.' Mesquite paused and looked at the bow proudly. 'I lived with 'em back when I first crossed the border to escape Stadtlander's rope.'

Drifter studied him curiously. 'You're a man of many

surprises, *amigo.*'

Mesquite grinned wickedly. 'That's what Ingrid says every time I make love to her.'

'Now you're bragging,' Drifter said. But he was smiling as he said it.

Moving carefully, as if in slow motion, they carried the box of dynamite down from the hayrack. Both men were sweating freely by the time they rested the box on the dirt floor and most of it wasn't because of the stifling heat.

'Wooof,' Mesquite said, wiping his forehead on his sleeve. 'That ain't somethin' I want to do on a regular basis.'

'Nor I,' said Drifter. 'It's not exactly going to be a fun ride from here to the stronghold, either. If that pack mule steps in a pothole or happens to trip and stumble along the way, there won't be enough of us left to bury.'

It was a grim, sobering thought.

CHAPTER EIGHTEEN

They rode on into the night, crossing a vast rock-strewn basin flanked by distant mountains, always heading west toward the Sierra Madre Occidental.

They rode in single file. Mesquite led the way, with Emily and Forbes following, and Drifter bringing up the rear. He'd taken it upon himself to lead the pack mule, carefully avoiding ruts as he picked the smoothest ground so that the animal wouldn't trip or stumble and blow them all to hell.

Coyotes howled and yapped in the darkness surrounding them, some close enough to make the horses nervous. Earlier bats had kept the insects away, but now the bats were gone, leaving the insects to whine about their faces.

Once, a family of Eva's Desert Mice darted in front of Drifter's horse, startling the temperamental sorrel so that it suddenly crab-stepped, almost unsaddling Drifter. Silently cursing, he reined up and soothed the horse until it stopped trembling, then gently urged it forward again.

'You all right back there?' Mesquite called.

'Yeah, yeah, I'm fine,' Drifter replied. He glanced back at the pack mule, which had remained remarkably unconcerned by the sorrel's behavior, and blessed it for its placid disposition. He then faced front again, his thud-thudding heart gradually calming.

Overhead, there was no moon but the cloudless, dark sky

was a glitter with stars. Black, jagged mountain peaks made up the horizon. A cold wind blew off the mountains. It came at them in sudden gusts, chilling the four riders, whipping them with a relentless ferocity equal to the scorching daytime heat.

Around nine o'clock they stopped to rest the horses, relieve themselves, and crunch down a hardtack cracker with a piece of jerky. Then, after a few sips of water, they mounted up and continued on under the bluish starlight.

'Ever wonder where the moon is on nights like this?' Forbes said, gazing skyward.

' 'Paches believe it's eaten by the sun,' Mesquite said. 'That's why when it reappears again it's called a new moon.'

'You are so full of it,' Drifter said, chuckling.

'He's also grammatically incorrect,' Emily said. 'When something reappears it means it appears again, so you don't need to say "reappears again". That's redundant.'

Deflated, Mesquite grumbled something about 'shootin' a fella full of holes with words' and then stopped talking so abruptly Drifter almost felt sorry for him.

'It may be redundant, whatever the hell that means,' Forbes grumbled, 'but it don't explain where the moon is when there ain't no clouds to hide it.'

'That's easy,' Emily said. 'The moon orbits the earth once a month so for a few days each month it's between us and the sun . . . and therefore we can't see it.'

'Jesus. . . .' Mesquite muttered softly.

'Is that true?' Forbes called back to Drifter. 'Or is she funnin' with me?'

'It's true,' Drifter replied. 'Now, all of you quit yapping so I can concentrate on keeping this horse from tripping and blowing us to kingdom come.'

They rode on in silence, the only sounds made by the horses' hoofs plodding over the hard, sandy ground.

*

It was midnight before they rested again. Each of them then wetted their kerchiefs from their canteens and wiped their own horses' lips before taking a few sips themselves. Then, munching on another cracker, they led their horses for a mile or so, the walking feeling good after sitting so many hours in the saddle.

When they finally remounted, Emily stifled a yawn and then asked Drifter if they were going to ride all night. 'Mostly,' he replied.

'Can you tell me why,' she said. He hesitated and reading his expression, she added: 'I have a right to know, Quint. I may be not much more than a child in your eyes, but it's my family that was killed and my horses that were stolen. And if things go wrong at the stronghold, I will be the one dying alongside you.'

He studied her, long and hard, as if seeing her as an adult for the first time. 'You're right,' he agreed. 'You are not a child and I'll try to remember that in future. We're riding all night,' he explained, 'because tomorrow we'll be crossing a desert called the Devil's Furnace—'

'*El Horno del Diablo*, yes, I've heard Pa speak of it. A land forsaken by God, he called it.'

' 'Cording to Gabe, that pretty much describes it. Anyway, he's crossed it several times and in his opinion the best way to do it is at night. So, way I figure it, by getting as close to it as possible by dawn then sleeping or resting until dusk, we should then be able to make it across in two nights without much trouble. You agree?'

'Heartily,' Emily said. She impulsively moved close and pecked him on the cheek. 'Thank you, Quint, for trusting me.'

'Wait,' Drifter said, grasping her reins before she could ride off. 'There's something else I should mention.'

'What?'

Lowering his voice so only she could hear, he said: 'A

little "fatherly" advice: It's good to be smart and know things that other folks may not be aware of. But sometimes, Emily, it's even smarter to hold back some of that knowledge, you know, so you don't sound like a know-it-all and rankle people by making them feel small.'

He expected her to be offended, but instead she nodded in agreement and said: 'Now you sound like Pa. He was always telling me the same thing. Said no matter how brainy I was, if I didn't know when to bite my tongue, I'd end up an old maid.'

Drifter grinned. 'I wouldn't fret over that,' he said gently. 'The chances of you winding up a spinster are about as likely as me getting hitched – which is no chance at all.' He dug his heels into the sorrel's flanks and rode off before she could ask him why.

CHAPTER NINETEEN

There are places on this earth that were not meant to be inhabited by any living creatures, including man.

El Horno del Diablo was one of them.

Stretching more than three hundred miles across its widest part down to sixty at its narrowest, it was a vast expanse of parched, sandy desert in which only the hardiest of plants and creatures managed to survive. Boulders and rocks littered it, scattered haphazardly as if thrown there by some bored giant. Jackrabbits existed along its borders and in the tall grasses that fringed the foothills fronting the various mountain ranges, and flocks of upland birds flew over it as they searched for more hospitable places to land or nest.

When the four of them came within sight of it, dawn was turning the dark sky to dove-gray. Imperceptibly, yet rapidly, the gray changed to violet and then finally to a pale primrose in which the stars gradually faded. The air was crackling-dry and already the approaching day was chasing the chill from the earth.

Making camp in a sandy hollow sheltered on three sides by strangely shaped, wind-eroded boulders, they unsaddled and watered the horses and the mule, and then turned them loose to nibble on anything edible they could find. To prevent them from straying, Drifter and Mesquite strung their ropes across the one opening between the boulders, while Emily and Forbes spread out the bedrolls and made pillows out of the saddles.

Honey mesquite and chamiso had somehow taken root in the hollow, as had several lechuguilla plants, known as 'shin-daggers' because of their long, tough, sharp leaves. Drifter put on his wrangler gloves and pulled out a handful of them.

'If you wake up and feel thirsty, chew on these,' he said, handing them out. 'There's water stored in the bulbs.'

Setting up camp had only taken a little while, but by the time they settled into their blankets it was already growing warm. Thirty minutes later, as the sun cleared the eastern mountain peaks, the heat increased until it became uncomfortably hot. Fortunately, none of them noticed it. Exhausted by the all-night ride, the four of them had fallen asleep almost immediately upon resting their heads on their saddles and closing their eyes.

The intense, suffocating heat woke them at midday. By then they had all discarded their blankets and their clothing was soaked in sweat. Because the sun was directly overhead there was no shade; worse, the giant boulders that formed a natural horseshoe around them, acted like a windbreak, shutting out any semblance of a breeze.

Realizing that the few sips of warm, metal-tasting water they were allowing themselves every hour would not prevent them from dehydrating, Drifter knew that if they were going to survive they had to find a way to protect themselves from the blazing sun. That's when his memory kicked in. Telling the others to follow him, he ducked under the ropes across the entrance and ventured out into the eye-achingly bright desert. There, about two hundred yards away, a clump of ocotillo grew along the banks of an arroyo. On reaching it, they cut off the longest, thickest branches and carried them back to the hollow where they used them as make-shift tent poles to support their blankets.

'It's not perfect,' he said as they crawled into the man-made shade, 'but it could mean the difference between living and dying.'

Mesquite shook his head. 'I hate to admit it, but I never would've thought of this. Not in a million moons.'

'Neither would I,' Drifter said, 'if I hadn't read a book about Bedouins.'

'Who?' Forbes said.

Emily, about to explain, remembered Drifter's advice and said nothing.

Drifter gave her a look to show how proud he was of her, then said: 'They're a tribe of Arabs, nomads who wander about the desert in Arabia. They wear these long loose robes and ride camels because, according to this book, camels can go days, even weeks without water.'

'Do tell,' Forbes said, interested. 'And these Arab fellas, they make shade same way we're doin'?'

'When they're not near their tents, yeah. There were lots of photographs in the book; one showed this Arab using a stick to hold part of his robe over his head as protection against the sun.'

'Be damned,' Mesquite said. Then to Emily: 'How come you didn't know 'bout these Arabs, smarty?'

'Just because I go to school,' she said demurely, 'doesn't mean I know everything.'

Forbes said: 'I ain't never had much use for books. But if you can learn stuff to keep you alive, I may have to give up whittlin' and start readin'.'

CHAPTER TWENTY

By mid-afternoon the boulders themselves formed spears of shade that added protection from the relentless sun. Drifter and the others, though drained by the merciless heat, managed to get valuable rest. An hour before dusk they crunched down two crackers and strips of beef jerky, sucked water from the remaining shoots of lechuguilla, and saddled their animals. Mesquite cautiously checked the dynamite. Drifter had kept the box under the shade beside him throughout the day and now, as Mesquite examined the top layer of sticks, he found them surprisingly free of crystals. He reburied them in the straw. He, Drifter and Forbes then gently strapped the box on the back of the pack mule, wedging a blanket under it to help lessen the jolting caused by the plodding motion of the animal.

Dusk fell, enveloping the desert in a waning violet light. It was still hot, but finally tolerable as the four set out across the Devil's Furnace. They rode in silence, hoping to conserve every bit of energy, and gradually the miles slipped behind them. The scenery never changed: endless, flat, sun-baked dirt, powdery in places where silvery wind-blown sand had gathered; rock-hard in others, and here and there clumps of straggly mesquite and ocotillo pushing up through the ground in defiance of nature's cruel conditions. There was no sign of life save for a lone eagle, drifting high above them on the thermals as it looked for its evening meal. Its hungry screeches occasionally drifted down to the four riders. But they paid the cries no mind, content to doze in their slow-rocking saddles. . . .

The horses seemed re-invigorated – especially the Morgan, which had bucked and tried to bite Mesquite as he attempted to saddle it – and Drifter did not call for a rest until almost midnight.

'We keep this up,' Mesquite said as they each sipped water from their canteens, 'we're only gonna have a short ride left tomorrow night.'

'How's that affect our plans?' Forbes inquired.

'It doesn't,' Drifter said. 'We still hole up during the day and attack after the sun goes down. We need the dark,' he explained. 'Everything is more confusing, more frightening when you can't see what's happening – or who's causing it. Hopefully, *El Carnicero* and his men will think they're being attacked by a large force and pull back, giving us time to get the horses.'

'I have a question,' Emily said. 'How are we going to explode the dynamite in the dark? We can't shoot what we can't see.'

'I'm way ahead of you,' Drifter said. 'We'll wait until they start their cooking fires. The light of the moon will do the rest.'

'What if the moon ain't out, like it wasn't last night?' Forbes said.

'It will be,' Drifter promised. 'I've been counting the days.'

'An' if you miscounted?' Mesquite said softly.

'We'll tie strips of cloth to the arrows and set fire to them. They won't burn for long, but long enough for us to see where they hit and to get a bead on the dynamite. That's all we'll need.'

*

Quietly impressed, Emily waited until Mesquite and Forbes had gone off to relieve themselves and then said to Drifter: 'You know an awful lot about a lot of different things.'

'For a wrangler, you mean?'

'Sorry. I didn't mean to be rude.'

Drifter softened, 'You weren't,' and rubbed his nose with his fist.

'I was just curious,' Emily said. 'I've known you for as long as I can remember and yet . . . well, truth is I don't really know you at all.'

'Would you like to?'

'That's a strange question.'

'These are strange circumstances.'

'And you're strangest of all,' she said boldly.

'Why do you say that?'

Emily didn't answer right away. She chewed at her nail, searching for the best way to explain herself, and finally said: 'You've always been a mystery to me, did you know that?'

'Never gave it much thought.'

'Why should you? All these years, I'll bet I was nothing more than an annoying little brat to you.'

'You'd lose that bet,' he grinned, adding: 'though I must admit there were times I wanted to spank the dust out of you.'

'You should've,' Emily said. 'Poor Pa, he loved me so much he never could, and I probably would've been better off for it. Well, anyway,' she added, 'you were. A mystery, I mean. Still are.'

'Why? Because I read books . . . have learned a few different things?'

'No. Because you risked your life to save my family, but wouldn't help me. Not even when I begged you—'

'Begged?' He snorted good-naturedly. 'Beg isn't a word you're familiar with, Emily.'

'All right, asked then. Call it what you like, you still wouldn't. Then after I went off and hired the sheriff, for no apparent reason you changed your mind and showed up with an outlaw, a gunfighter who's ducking a rope. Goodness knows how, or why, but you managed to persuade him to help us and then without asking anyone, took charge of things. Sheriff Forbes, who barely knew you and is used to giving orders, respected you enough not to argue with you, even though because of his friendship with Pa, he had more reason to worry about me than you—'

'Maybe.'

'What did you say?'

He hesitated, for an instant wondering if he should tell her everything, but decided against it. 'Nothing. Go on.'

'Next thing I know, you save our lives back in Blanco Canyon and today, when we were almost dying from the heat, you found a way to save us again.'

He stopped her. 'What exactly is it you're trying to say, Emily?'

'I . . . I'm not sure.' She paused, confused, and watched as he rubbed his nose with his fist. Then: 'I just have this strange feeling about you, as if there was a reason you showed up at the ranch all these years.'

He shrugged. 'I liked your folks.'

'No other reason?'

'I liked your folks,' he repeated.

'And they liked you; especially Momma. Did you know that?'

He didn't want to lie, so he kept silent.

'She did, you know. She *really* liked you.'

'Emily,' Drifter chided, 'I know you mean well, but you're too young to know how—'

'—she felt? No, no, that's where you're wrong, Mr Quint Longley. Momma and I were best friends. She told me everything; all about how she grew up, met Pa, and lots of other things, personal things, woman stuff she said she couldn't tell Pa or my brothers 'cause, being men, they wouldn't understand. And one of them was that she cared about you—'

'Emily—'

'—enough to trust you . . . enough to tell *me* to trust you.'

'Emily, that's enough!'

'Know what else she told me? She said that if Pa hadn't come along first, she—'

'Dammit, girl, button your mouth!' He paused, teeth gritted, then said: 'Your folks are dead. Try to respect that – *and* your mother's confidences!'

His anger jolted her; shamed her. Tears stung her eyes.

'I'm s-sorry. You're right. I shouldn't have told you those things. They were secrets and . . . it's just . . . sometimes I feel like I have no one in the world to talk to and it scares me . . . makes me wonder what's going to happen to me. . . .' She broke off, tears spilling down her cheeks.

Drifter melted. 'Don't,' he begged. 'P-please don't cry . . . I— Here,' he dug out his kerchief and dabbed her tears away. 'You mustn't be scared. I'll look after you, keep you safe . . . always. You got my word on it.' He started to put his arms around her but guilt, or something close to it, wouldn't let him and instead he pressed his hands over hers and squeezed them fondly.

Comforted, Emily sniffed back her tears, then gazed up into his weathered face and smiled bravely. 'You were right all along,' she admitted. 'I am just a child . . .a silly little schoolgirl trying to act all grown up—'

'Emily, I—'

'No, no, it's all right,' she assured him. 'During the last few days I've had lots of time to think, to get to know myself . . . to realize how sheltered I've been at school and how, like you said, being smart isn't enough, not nearly enough, not if I want to grow up and get along in the world.'

'That's all part of being fourteen—'

'I didn't realize it back then,' she said, continuing as if he hadn't spoken, 'nor on the train coming to Santa Rosa. Wasn't till I was at the cemetery . . . saw Momma and Pa and my brothers being put in the ground, that I first felt it . . . first knew that things were different; that my life had changed and would never be the same. Of course I wouldn't admit it to myself then. I was too frightened . . . too alone. I thought if I kept denying it, maybe – just maybe everything would be all right again.'

'It will be,' Drifter promised. 'We'll get your horses back and I'll help you get the ranch running properly again—'

She stopped him. 'Thank you, that's very kind of you. But I've given the ranch to the sheriff for helping me and I intend to sell the horses and use the money to go back to school. I've always wanted to teach and now that I have no one, there's no reason to come back to Santa Rosa. Don't you agree?'

'Definitely,' he said, hoping he sounded convinced.

'Will you write to me?'

'Every chance I get.'

'No, I'm serious.'

'So am I.'

'Promise?'

'With bells on.'

She laughed and impulsively hugged him. It felt wonderful to have her arms around him, but he quickly warned himself not to get used to it. He knew it would only hurt more when he had to say goodbye.

CHAPTER TWENTY-ONE

They rode on into the ever-cooling darkness. They were four abreast now with Drifter out on the left flank, still leading the plodding, ever-placid pack mule. The coolness was good for the dynamite, Mesquite had told them, because there was less chance of the sticks sweating and therefore less chance of a nitroglycerin crystal forming and causing an explosion. Still, there was always that chance and though the farther they rode without mishap, the better their chances were of surviving, not one of them didn't cringe inwardly when the mule happened to kick a stone or step in a rut and stumble.

Ahead, in the far distance, the black, majestic, towering peaks of the Sierra Madre Occidental seemed to reach up clear to the stars. Looking at them as she rode Emily wanted to ask if they had to climb those peaks. But she didn't. She was afraid either Drifter or Mesquite might say yes.

Night gradually faded into those cold, lonely hours prior to dawn. And still they rode onward, saddles creaking, their breath fogging before their faces, hoof-beats monotonously thudding on the sandy dirt.

The mountains finally drew closer, close enough that the riders could see the foothills in front of them. They were a grim, forbidding sight and with dawn less than an hour away, they grew more visible by the minute. They were steep, wooded, rock-studded hills, slashed by deep canyons covered by dense brush, making it easy to understand why the Comancheros had chosen this rugged terrain in which to build their stronghold.

'How close do you want to get?' Mesquite asked, reining up.

'I'll leave that up to you,' Drifter said. 'You know where the stronghold is. Just make sure it's somewhere we won't be detected once the sun comes up.'

They reached the hills shortly before dawn. A silvery wafer-moon hung in the gray, cloudy sky, offering little light to the riders as they rode through the trees fringing the lower slopes. Though Drifter didn't say anything, he hoped that tomorrow's moon would be brighter or it would be of no help to them.

Not long after they crossed the tree-line the hillside grew steeper and they found great slabs of stone piled haphazardly on either side of the narrow twisting trail. As they rode between them, Mesquite explained that the Raramuri originally believed the giant stones were part of the steps that their god, *Onoruame* used when he descended from heaven. That angered the Jesuits, who were forcing Christianity on the tribes, and they tried to make the Indians understand that an earthquake had hurled the stones there. But the Raramuri wouldn't listen. Many of them grew angry and attacked the local mission, killing all the Jesuits there. The Spanish Church retaliated by torturing the Raramuri until they denied their pagan gods, then crucified them and lined the trails with their bodies as a warning to any future heathen worshipers.

'That's a strange way to introduce Jesus into their lives,'

Emily said, thinking aloud. 'Especially since the Bible says "love thy neighbor".'

No one answered her. The horrific image was depressing, and none of them spoke again as they followed Mesquite deeper into the hills.

The trail soon became lost in dense brush. It made the going slow and tough, and it was daylight when Mesquite finally led them into a tiny secluded clearing hidden from above by stunted, leafy blue oaks and bushes growing out of cracks in the boulders. They were now only a short ride away from Lobo Canyon, where the Comancheros' stronghold was located, but Mesquite assured the others that he'd holed up here many times and they were in no danger of being seen by either lookouts or *El Carnicero*'s patrols.

A thin waterfall cascaded down between the rocks, forming a shallow pool at the edge of the clearing. The sight of the sparkling, tumbling water was enticing after days of searing heat and desert, and quickly dismounting, they let their animals drink while they waded in up to their knees and splashed the refreshingly cold water over themselves.

Afterward, they kicked off their boots to let them dry in the sun and spread their bedrolls under a flat overhanging rock. It jutted out several feet and was wide enough to offer all of them a few hours of shade. Everyone was hungry and looking forward to breakfast. But Drifter insisted they not light a fire, for fear of alerting the Comancheros, and therefore forcing them to go without coffee or hot beans. Instead they ate hardtack and jerky – again! Emily was so sick of both she could barely swallow her food. Forbes wasn't much better. He was addicted to black coffee, and without his daily 'fix' became ill-tempered and bristly. He also never stopped complaining. The others put up with it for a while, but finally Mesquite snapped.

'Shut up, old man,' he said. 'I'm sick of your damn' belly-achin'.'

Both had removed their gun-belts before entering the pool, and now the ex-lawman, knowing he had twenty pounds on the outlaw, came at Mesquite, fists clenched.

'Why don't you shut me up?' he challenged.

'Happily,' Mesquite said. Jumping up, he lowered his head and rammed Forbes in the belly. Wind knocked out of him, the big man went sprawling. Mesquite dived on top of him and began punching him with both hands.

Alarmed, Emily jumped up, shouting: 'Stoppit! You hear me? Stop—'

Drifter, who'd been filling his canteen under the water-fall when the fight started, brushed her aside and knocked Mesquite off the ex-lawman.

'Cut it out, you damn fool!' Without pausing he turned, saw that Forbes was scrambling up, ready to fight, and swung his canteen at the former sheriff. Like a roundhouse right, it caught Forbes on the temple. Momentarily stunned, he collapsed in a heap.

Drifter quickly turned back Mesquite, who was buckling on his gun-belt. Stepping between the outlaw and Forbes, Drifter told him to calm down, adding: 'We've all come too far and endured too much for it to end like this.'

'Get out of my way,' Mesquite hissed.

'Dammit, listen to me, will you? You thumb that hammer and you'll bring the Comancheros down on us.' He looked meaningfully at Emily before asking: 'You know what they'll do to her? Want that on your conscience?'

Mesquite hesitated, hand hovering above his holstered six-gun, and then slowly regained control. Stepping to one side of Drifter, he glared at Forbes.

'When this is over, old man, you see me comin' you'd better fill your hand, 'cause I intend to kill you.' Turning, he ducked under the rocky overhang and stretched out on his blanket.

'Button it,' Drifter told Forbes as he started to speak. 'You already used up your nine lives!'

CHAPTER TWENTY-TWO

The moon was bright that night, as Drifter had hoped, but it was covered by slow-moving clouds. *Win some, lose some,* he thought as he, Emily and Forbes followed Mesquite up the steep winding trail that led over the hilltop and down into Lobo Canyon. Visibility was poor in the darkness; he could just make out the steep slopes of the surrounding hills and the silhouettes of their lumpy peaks against the overcast sky. He also hoped that he'd been right about the Comancheros' cooking fires offering enough light to see where the arrows carrying the dynamite landed; otherwise they'd have to use valuable time to tie strips of cloth to the arrows and then light them – all the while worrying about being spotted by any of the lookouts.

It was slow going and dangerous in the dark and thirty minutes had slipped by before Drifter, Mesquite, Emily and Forbes finally rode over the crest of the hill. Reining up, they looked down at the Comancheros' sprawling strong-hold. Drifter sighed with relief. As he'd predicted, the glow of cooking fires illuminated the camp. Heavily armed men moved about the area, while their women prepared the evening meal and children played in the dirt, all totally unaware of the fact that they were being watched.

Indicating the weathered shacks and outbuildings that were scattered throughout the front half of the canyon, Drifter asked Mesquite if he knew which one of them belonged to *El Carnicero*. The outlaw shook his head, explaining that a lot of changes had taken place since he'd holed up here. 'There were no barricades or shacks back then. The Comancheros lived in caves in the cliffs and—'

'Look!' Emily, who'd been staring fixedly at the corrals, suddenly pointed at the farthest one. 'Over there! I think those are my mares!'

Drifter handed her his field glasses, saying: 'Here . . . make sure.'

Adjusting the lenses, she trained the glasses on the corral. 'Yes . . . yes definitely . . . they're mine. But I can't see Diablo anywhere.'

'Maybe they've sold him?' Forbes said.

'Let's not jump to conclusions,' Drifter said as Emily looked dejected. 'We'll find out soon enough when we bust in there. Most important thing right now is to figure out where *El Carnicero* is; we get him and it's gonna take a lot of the fight out of his men.'

Mesquite had been looking at the far end of the canyon. Asking Drifter to give him the field glasses, he trained them on an adobe house barely visible against the canyon wall. 'Beano!' he said softly.

'What?' Drifter asked. 'What d'you see?'

Mesquite returned the glasses. 'There,' he pointed. 'That's where the sonofabitch lives. Bet my saddle on it.'

As Drifter trained the glasses on the building, Emily looked curiously at Mesquite. 'How do you know about Beano?'

'Met this fella once from New Orleans – Monsewer somethin' or other. Had this game he'd brung with him from France; bunch of little white balls and cards with numbers. You marked the numbers an' if they matched up with the balls, you yelled out Bean—'

He stopped as Drifter tucked the binoculars away, saying: 'If you're right, and I think you are, we'll hit them from the other end of the canyon.'

'Why?' Emily asked.

'It's closer to *El Carnicero* and your mares. It's also farther from his men.' Drifter indicated the scattered shacks. 'Which means we have more time, if only a few minutes, to get in, grab the horses and Cordero—'

'Who?'

'Bacilio Cordero – that's *El Carnicero*'s real name.'

'Why don't we just shoot the bastard?' Forbes said.

' 'Cause, alive – a hostage – he's our ticket out of here. Can your bow reach those shacks from the other end?' he added to Mesquite.

'Uh-uh. Not with the arrows weighted down with dynamite. I could reach 'em from here or up on those cliffs, though. I could also shoot 'em from up there. That way the explosions will keep everyone busy while you're takin' care of *El Carnicero*.'

'I dunno,' said Drifter. 'Something goes wrong and we can't get to him, you'd be hung out to dry.'

'I'll take that chance,' Mesquite said. 'But it's your call.'

CHAPTER
TWENTY-THREE

It took Drifter, Emily and Forbes almost an hour to ride around the perimeter of the canyon. They moved cautiously, ever wary of being seen by one of the many lookouts that continuously circled the area, and finally reached the west entrance. By then Mesquite had hidden his horse among the trees and brush that grew right up to the base of the cliff, and scrambled his way up the steep rocky slope, almost to the top.

Once there, he strung his bow, took a hunting arrow from the doe-skin quiver slung over his back, and notched it on the string. Waiting until the lookout had his back to him, Drifter took careful aim and shot.

The 'twang' of the bowstring caused the lookout to half-turn toward the sound, but before he could make out Mesquite's kneeled silhouette, the arrow struck him in the neck, the sharp-edged arrowhead severing his jugular. The lookout dropped his rifle, made a faint gurgling sound, sank to his knees, and then pitched forward on to his face. Dead.

Mesquite scrambled up the last few feet to the summit and ran to the corpse. Removing his hat, he replaced it with the lookout's black, flat-crowned Stetson. Then pulling the arrow out of the dead man's throat, he returned it to his quiver and rolled the corpse over the edge. It bounced from rock to rock, limbs flopping, and finally came to rest between two boulders. Ducked low, the outlaw then hurried to the inner edge of the cliff and took cover behind some bushes overlooking the stronghold. There, he pulled a handful of arrows from the quiver and leaned them against the rock beside him. Each shaft had a stick of dynamite tied to it by a thin strip formed out of shredded ocotillo leaves. Next he checked his bowstring, rubbing it between finger and thumb, feeling for any broken strands. Finding none, he leaned the weapon alongside the arrows, tucked a pinch of snuff inside his cheek and leaned back to await Drifter's signal.

The west entrance to the canyon was fronted by a broad stretch of dirt that had been cleared of trees and brush. It was seldom used by the Comancheros, who almost exclusively entered and left by the north-east entrance. Hence, there was only one lookout, and he sat dozing on a flat rock some twenty feet above the barricade. A large boulder was roped to one end of the barricade, as a counterbalance, while the opposite end was fastened down by a stout cross-branch lodged among the lower rocks. Another rope was fastened to the branch, and then it stretched up to the lookout.

Drifter, crouched behind the rocks at the edge of the clearing, admired the simplicity: upon a signal all the lookout had to do was yank on the rope, releasing the cross-branch so that the barricade raised on its own, allowing the Comancheros to escape any attackers.

Signaling to Emily and Forbes – who stood with the horses and the mule behind some trees – to stay put, Drifter began to wriggle on his belly toward the barricade. Halfway there he heard the lookout stirring and froze. But the man was merely stretching, and after a huge yawn, continued dozing. Drifter reached the barricade unnoticed, slowly stood up, and hurled his hunting knife at the lookout. The knife buried itself in the man's chest. Shocked, he tried to stand, hands clutching the handle of the knife, and then dropped. He rolled off the flat rock and landed, face-down, on to the barricade, impaled by one of the pointed logs. He died instantly.

Drifter signaled to Emily and Forbes. Both joined him with the horses. Drifter took out a strip of cloth, scratched a match against the rocks and lit the cloth. He waved it over his head, signaling to Mesquite to start shooting. Then dousing the flame he turned to the others, said calmly: 'Now, remember, watch where Gabe's arrows land but don't fire at them unless I give the signal. Clear?'

Emily and Forbes nodded. All three moved close to the barricade and looked between the roped logs, waiting for the fireworks to begin.

Shortly, they saw an arrow come arcing down off the top of the cliff. It landed in one of the cooking fires, causing a shower of sparks, and exploded.

People gathered about the fire were blown skyward.

Women and children everywhere screamed.

Men, once over the shock of the explosion, ran for their weapons.

Instant chaos.

'Now why the hell didn't I think of that?' Drifter muttered grimly.

'Who knew the sonofabitch could shoot that good?' Forbes said.

Emily started to scold him for cursing but her words were lost in another explosion as a second arrow landed in another cooking fire, causing the same results. This time flaming coals flew everywhere. Some landed on top of the wooden shacks, which quickly began to burn.

Drifter waited no longer. Pulling on the rope tied to the cross-branch, he moved back as the barricade quickly swung upward. Leaving the pack mule tied to a tree, all three mounted and spurred their horses into the canyon.

Mesquite, meanwhile, fired three more arrows. The first landed in a cooking fire, instantly exploding; each of the others landed in a shack. Quickly, before the noise of the explosion faded, he took aim with his Winchester, snapped off two shots, and grinned as two more explosions followed. The shacks were blown to pieces.

Behind one of them was a shed. It contained kegs of gunpowder, ammo and dynamite. It suddenly erupted, the thundering explosion echoing off the cliffs. Flames and debris shot a hundred feet in the air, briefly illuminating the entire canyon.

The Comancheros, the explosions hiding the noise of Mesquite's rifle, were confused as to where their enemy was hidden. Desperate, they took cover behind the rocks scattered about the canyon, but could find no targets to shoot at.

Before the shed exploded, Drifter, Emily and Forbes had already reached the adobe house. Drifter waved them on and sprang from the saddle in time to see three young, half-naked Mexican women rush out the door. Panicked by the explosions, they didn't notice Drifter and fled in different directions.

Moments later a short muscular man emerged, shirtless and still pulling on one boot. Darkly handsome with cruel dark eyes, he suddenly saw Drifter standing before him, rifle in hand, and to his credit dived back into the house.

Drifter ran to the house, flattened himself against the wall and peered around the door. Immediately, shots were fired, driving him back. Cursing that he hadn't been able to force the Comanchero leader to surrender while out in the open, Drifter glanced toward the corrals. Emily and Forbes had already reached the one containing her mares and were now herding them back toward him.

Waiting until another explosion had blown up the water tower, Drifter yelled into the doorway:

'Cordero! You hear me?'

No answer.

'Bacilio Cordero, do you hear me?'

Still no answer.

Drifter said: 'You got ten seconds to throw out your gun and walk out after it. Otherwise, the next stick of dynamite is going to blow you and this place to hell! Ten . . . nine . . . eight. . . .'

He broke off as something small rolled out of the doorway.

Instinctively, almost before he saw it was a hand grenade, Drifter dived sideways, rolled as he hit the dirt, and crab-crawled behind the side of the house. Even so, the explosion made his ears ring as dirt and stones flew past him.

He vaguely heard laughter, followed by hurried, limping footsteps, and realized too late that Cordero had ran out through the door.

As Drifter scrambled to his feet, rifle in hand, shots rang out. Then he heard the pounding of galloping horses. Running to the front of the house, he saw the Comancheros' leader trying to get out of the way of a herd of horses stampeding toward him. They were urged on by Emily and Forbes, shouting as they rode behind the fifteen mares.

It was then that Drifter noticed Cordero had been shot in his right leg. His pant leg was ripped open, revealing a blood-stained bandage that had come unwound and now trailed in the dirt. Realizing he would be trampled by the onrushing mares, Drifter grabbed Cordero from behind and dragged him aside. Both went sprawling. Moments later the horses galloped past, followed by Emily and Forbes.

Dust swirled around the two men on the ground. Taking advantage of it, Cordero smashed Drifter in the face with his elbow, then rose and pulled his knife. Momentarily dazed, Drifter saw the blade flash in the light of the burning shacks and rolled backward. Cordero stabbed empty air. And before he could recover, Drifter jumped up, grabbed his rifle and clubbed him across the face. *El Carnicero* grunted, staggered back and, unable to support himself on his wounded leg, collapsed.

Drifter dragged him up, and turned him to face the Comancheros who were now angrily charging toward them.

'Tell 'em to back off,' Drifter said, jamming his rifle in Cordero's ribs, 'or watch you die.'

'You kill me, *gringo*, you die as well.'

'That suits me,' Drifter said. 'I never figured on growing old anyway.' He jammed the rifle harder into Cordero's side. 'Make the call.'

El Carnicero hesitated, then gestured to his men and shouted orders in Spanish. They grudgingly halted, lowered their weapons, and glared at Drifter.

'Surrender,' Cordero told Drifter, 'and I will let you live, *gringo*.'

Drifter glanced behind him and saw that Emily and Forbes had herded the mares out of the canyon and were now waiting, rifles ready, in the entrance.

'*Gracias*, but I got other plans for you. Now, move.' He supported *El Carnicero* under his right arm and stepped backward, bringing his prisoner with him.

The Comancheros moved forward a step, threateningly, ready to shoot Drifter at their leader's command.

Drifter continued to march Cordero backward, a step at a time, never taking his eyes off the Comancheros, until he reached his horse. The irascible sorrel chose that moment to act up. Side-stepping as Drifter reached for the reins, it tried to cow-kick him.

Drifter jumped back, barely avoiding the kick. Then, controlling the urge to shoot the goddamn animal, he gritted his teeth, said, 'Easy, boy . . . easy,' and again reached for the reins. This time the sorrel stood still. Reins in hand, Drifter kept his grip on Cordero's arm, his eyes fixed on the Comancheros, and began walking backward toward the entrance.

'Don't worry, partner,' Forbes called out behind him. 'We got you covered.'

Drifter waved his thanks and continued walking backward, bringing Cordero and the sorrel with him.

The frustrated Comancheros pressed forward, cutting the gap between themselves and Drifter.

'Tell them that's far enough,' Drifter said to Cordero. 'Do it!' he ordered when Cordero remained silent. '*Pronto!*'

El Carnicero gave an ugly laugh. '*Sí . . . sí . . .* I will tell them, *puerco yanqui*. But it does not change anything. My men will follow you and find you . . . all of you . . . and then, when you are roasting over a fire, you will beg me for a quick death.'

'You know,' Drifter drawled, 'you're starting to get on my nerves.' He clubbed Cordero with his rifle, caught him as he fell, and in the same motion swung the wounded man across his saddle. It was done so quickly that it was over before the Comancheros could stop him. Drifter then tucked his rifle into its scabbard, mounted, drew his six-gun, and aimed it at Cordero's head.

'You want *El Carnicero* to live,' he said to the Comancheros, 'do not follow us.'

A tall, greasy-haired man holding a shotgun, growled: '*Usted no puede matar todos nosotros, gringo.*'

'I don't *have* to kill all of you. Just him.' Drifter thumbed back the hammer of his Colt. 'Any takers?'

The Comancheros hesitated, uneasy, no one wanting to be the one responsible for their leader's death.

'*Dónde le llevan?*' demanded a hulking, bearded man.

'To *El horno del Diablo*. There, if we're not followed, I will release him. *Entiende?*'

No one moved. No one spoke.

'Entiende?' Drifter repeated.

Grudgingly, the Comancheros nodded. '*Sí. Nosotros entendemos.*'

Drifter wheeled his horse around. 'Let's go,' he told Emily and Forbes, 'before they change their minds.'

'But what about Diablo,' Emily protested. 'I can't leave here without him.'

'Is he in one of the other corrals?'

'No, but—'

'Means they probably sold him on their way down here.'

'You don't know that!'

'No. But a stallion with his blood lines would bring a big price – big enough they couldn't turn it down. I'm sorry,' he said as Emily's face fell. 'I know how much Diablo means to you. But you got the mares; you'll just have to settle for that.'

'No, I—'

'He's right, missy,' Forbes said as Emily balked. 'We gotta get out of here. Bastards are gonna rush us any minute. Now, c'mon!' Slapping her mount on the rump with his hat, he kicked up his own horse and rode after her.

Drifter faced the angry Comancheros, 'Remember what I said. I see anyone following us and I'll shoot *El Carnicero*.' Then he turned and spurred his horse away.

CHAPTER TWENTY-FOUR

From behind the rocks on top of the cliff Mesquite had watched the drama unfolding in the canyon below him. His dynamite-laden arrows and pinpoint shooting had caused fear and chaos among the Comancheros, who seemed bewildered by an enemy they couldn't see. As shack after shack exploded, they scattered in panic and ran for cover. By the time it dawned on them that the shooter was positioned atop one of the cliffs, their camp was a mass of flames, their leader had been captured, and the fight was basically over.

Looking on, Mesquite made sure Drifter, Emily, and Forbes had safely ridden away with Cordero, now astride the pack mule, and the mares before unstringing his bow and descending the outer slope of the cliff. Overhead the moon appeared briefly between the drifting clouds, brightening the cool darkness around him. As he carefully picked his way down between the rocks, he marveled at how comparatively easy it had been to capture *El Carnicero* and defeat his men – so easy, in fact, that he suddenly felt a twinge of uneasiness, as if this were the proverbial calm before the storm. He tried to shake it off. But it lingered stubbornly and as he neared the base of the cliff he stopped, protected by a rock, and pumped a round into his rifle. He waited there for a few moments, listening intently for any sounds of approaching danger. But the night remained quiet save for the yip-yipping of a distant coyote and an occasional faint noise made by some tiny creature scurrying through the brush below. Chiding himself for being overly cautious, Mesquite continued his descent, dirt and shale slithering ahead of him.

On reaching the base of the cliff he paused a moment to remember where he'd hidden his horse and then, shouldering his bow and Winchester, he hurried through the trees and brush toward it.

He'd only taken a few steps when two Comanchero lookouts jumped out from behind the boulders in front of him, rifles aimed at his belly.

'Hold it right there!' the bigger of the two snarled.

Before the man had finished speaking Mesquite, his cat-quick reflexes honed by constantly being on the run, instinctively hurled himself forward. In the same instant, while still falling, he snatched his Colt from its holster and fired twice before he hit the ground.

Both Comancheros staggered back, eyes bugged, blood slowly welling from a bullet hole in each man's chest. The smaller man dropped his rifle and sank to his knees, already dead, and pitched on to his face. The other man, almost as massive as a bear, sustained life long enough to squeeze the trigger of his Steyr Mannlicher bolt-action rifle, then took a few staggering steps before collapsing.

But Mesquite never saw this happen. He was already unconscious.

Twenty minutes later, Drifter and the others reined up at their rendezvous site – a rocky outcrop circled by gnarly, twisted blue oaks – and looked around for Mesquite. Seeing no sign of him, they remained in their saddles and waited anxiously for the outlaw to arrive.

Fifteen minutes passed. Still no Mesquite Jennings.

'Dammit, he should've been here by now,' Drifter said.

'How long we gonna wait?' Forbes asked.

'Long as it takes.'

Beside them *El Carnicero*, now conscious and astride the pack mule with his ankles roped under the animal's belly, grinned mockingly. '*Bueno*,' he said. 'It is good that you wait. More time for my men to catch up with you.'

'*Cállate!*' Drifter told him.

Cordero shut up, but his smirk enraged Emily.

'My stallion,' she demanded. 'Where is he?'

'Ah, *sí*, the stallion . . . *un animal más bello, señorita.*'

'Never mind how beautiful he is; what did you do with him?'

'Do, *señorita?* Why, we eat him of course. . .' Cordero laughed cruelly. '*La carne es muy sabrosa.*'

Emily lost it. Spurring her horse alongside the Comancheros' leader, she began whipping him across the face with her reins.

'Butcher!' she screamed at him. 'Murdering, butchering bastard!'

'Hey, hey, hey. . . .' Drifter quickly wedged the sorrel between her horse and the pack mule, driving her back. 'That's enough!'

'I want him dead,' she hissed. 'Dead, dead, dead!'

'I know, I know,' Drifter said gently. 'We all do. But you mustn't let him get under your skin. We need him alive if we're to get out of here safely.'

'But you said you'd let him go when we reached the Devil's Furnace. I heard you!'

'We'll cross that creek when we come to it,' Drifter said.

'I'll shoot him if you let him go,' Emily sobbed. 'I swear I will.'

Before Drifter could reply, Cordero, welts reddening his face, grinned at Emily. 'You had better do it now, *señorita*, before my men arrive.'

'*Cállate!*' Drifter told him. 'Or, goddammit, I'll shoot you myself.'

But instead of shutting up Cordero laughed and said: 'I like that you show such fire, *señorita.* Tonight, before my men and I rape you, I will make you dance naked for me and—'

Forbes, who'd ridden close to Cordero while he was talking, back-handed him across the face. It was a stunning blow and *El Carnicero* slumped over the horse's neck.

'Sorry.' Forbes shrugged apologetically at Drifter. 'I couldn't have the sonofabitch talkin' 'bout Miss Emily like that.'

'Forget it,' Drifter said. 'I was on the verge of shooting him myself.' He looked up as the moon appeared whitely from behind the clouds. 'Can't figure out what's taking Gabe this long. He's way overdue.'

'Think somethin's happened to him?'

Drifter shrugged, unwilling to say what he was really thinking. 'Tell you what,' he said to Forbes and Emily. 'Why don't you two ride ahead while I look around? Maybe Gabe twisted his ankle or something—'

'You don't believe that for a second,' Emily said, adding: 'I say we all either stay and look for Mesquite or we all leave together. One or the other.'

'No, Drifter's right,' Forbes broke in. 'You gotta go, Miss Emily. Now! 'Fore these bastards get it into their heads to come after us. But it's me who has to stay,' he said to Drifter.

'Why you?'

' 'Cause you can look after her better; offer her more protection than me. You can see that, can't you? Hell's fire, I'm a piddlin' shot at best and you know it. Then there's my age. Like you and Mesquite are always remindin' me, I'm an old man. I ain't even sure I can make it back across that goddamn desert, an' then where the hell would she be?'

128

Drifter hesitated, knowing Forbes was right . . . but. . . .

'I don't know why we're arguin' about this anyway,' Forbes continued. 'We're wastin' time. I mean, it ain't like me an' Mesquite plan on takin' up squatters' rights. We'll be along shortly. Might even catch up with you 'fore you ride out of the hills.'

'All right,' Drifter said, suddenly deciding. 'But don't spend too much time looking for Gabe. For all we know he was forced to skin out of here.'

'Don't worry, I'll be along soon,' Forbes said. He smiled at Emily, adding: ' 'Case we don't hook up again for a spell, I want you to know somethin'. If I'd ever had a daughter, missy, I would've wanted her to be just like you.'

'Thank you, Lonnie.' Fighting tears, Emily rode up to him, leaned over, and pecked him on the cheek. 'And thanks for being such a true friend to Pa.'

As she rode off, Forbes said to Drifter: 'Make sure you get that little gal home safely, y'hear? 'Cause if'n you don't, I'll haunt you for the rest of your days.'

Drifter grinned and offered the big ex-sheriff his hand. '*Vaya con Dios, amigo.*'

CHAPTER TWENTY-FIVE

Forbes rode slowly through the trees and brush looking for Mesquite. The night sky was clear of clouds now and the moon hung like a great silvery orb in the darkness. By its light the former sheriff checked the ground and bushes for any signs of the outlaw; a bloodstained leaf, a piece of clothing snagged on a branch, a trail of blood . . . anything.

He found nothing.

Now and then he heard distant shouting and once a few shots were fired. Guessing it was the Comancheros arguing about whether or not they should pursue the *gringos*, Forbes knew that time was running out. Kneeing his horse closer to the base of the cliffs, he suddenly heard a groan nearby. He instantly reined up, dismounted, and began searching the bushes. 'Mesquite,' he called. 'That you?'

No reply.

'Mesquite! It's Lonnie Forbes . . . where are you?'

They were the last words he spoke.

A machete, swung from behind him by one of the perimeter lookouts, split his skull and Forbes crumpled without a sound.

Another Comanchero stepped out from the trees and joined the lookout, who jerked his machete free and spat on Forbes's corpse. '*Apestoso yanqui!*'

'We must find his friend,' the Comanchero said, poking the bushes with his rifle. 'The man he was lookin' for.'

'*Amigos,*' a voice behind them said. 'I'm right here.'

The two Comancheros whirled around to find Mesquite facing them, Colt in hand. They froze.

Mesquite smiled faintly, 'Mustn't keep hell waitin',' and shot them both.

For a moment he stood there, swaying slightly, blood caked around the bullet crease on his temple, and then he hunkered down beside Forbes's corpse.

The distant shouting grew louder then suddenly stopped, as if the argument was over. Excited cries followed, warning Mesquite that the Comancheros were on the move.

'Sorry I don't have time to bury you, *compadre,*' he told the corpse. 'You feel like it, you can cuss me out next time we meet.' Rising, he untied the all-black Morgan from a tree, stepped into the saddle, grabbed the reins of Forbes's horse and rode off.

CHAPTER TWENTY-SIX

The mares, all fifteen of them, came busting down the final hillside, followed by a swirling rooster-tail of dust. Choking on that dust was Emily, kerchief knotted over her face, herding the mares as skillfully as any cowboy as she guided her horse down the steep, treacherous slope.

Right behind her rode Drifter, one hand gripping the reins, the other the rope attached to the pack mule carrying *El Carnicero*. The leader of the Comancheros still had his feet roped under the belly of the mule, but now his hands were also tied and he was gagged to prevent him from giving away their position. Every so often Drifter looked back to see if they were being pursued. But so far, with the vast moonlit desert stretched out below, none of the Comancheros had caught up to them.

Finally they reached the bottom, the now gently sloping land leveling off as it became rock-strewn scrubland. Drifter removed Cordero's gag but did not untie his hands or feet. Ahead, Emily spurred her horse out in front of the mares, calling to them, coaxing them to slow down, until at last she had them stopped. Nostrils flared, chests heaving, flanks lathered in sweat, they stood milling around, snorting and nickering.

'Good work,' Drifter said as he rode up beside Emily.

'But let's keep them moving.'

'They need a blow,' she said.

'Later. They'll have plenty of time to rest once the sun comes up.'

Behind him Cordero laughed mockingly.

'Do not worry about the sun, *gringo*. You will not live to see it.'

They turned as he spoke and saw in the distance, a bunch of Comancheros riding down the nearest hillside.

'Don't count on it,' Drifter said. Then, dismounting, he told Emily: 'Go on. I'll catch up with you.'

'No. If we're going to stop them, we'll do it together. Don't argue,' she said as he started to protest. 'I'm not losing you too.' Dismounting, she pulled her rifle from its boot and levered a round into the chamber.

Drifter did the same. He then took the last four sticks of dynamite left in the pack mule's saddle-bags and hurled them as far as he could toward the hills. They landed some sixty feet away, clearly visible in the moonlight.

Leaving the mares where they stood, Drifter and Emily led their horses and the pack mule behind some nearby rocks. They weren't large enough to hide the animals, but offered cover to Drifter and Emily as they hunkered down behind them.

'You take the two on the left,' Drifter said, indicating the dynamite.

Emily nodded and, resting her rifle atop a rock, took careful aim.

'You are wasting your time,' Cordero sneered to Drifter. 'Dynamite will not stop my men.'

'We'll see,' Drifter replied. 'But if it doesn't, know this: killing you will be one of the sweet moments of my life.'

'Wait for my signal,' Drifter told Emily as they watched the twenty-odd Comancheros riding across the flatland toward them. 'Then take your time, hold your breath, and gently squeeze the trigger.'

She nodded, never taking her eye off the rifle sight. Inside she was trembling but somehow she managed to control her fear and in her heart she knew that she could do this.

The Comancheros rode ever-closer to the four sticks of dynamite.

'Now,' Drifter said softly. He waited for her to shoot, not wanting to break her concentration, and a moment later she fired; the stick lying farthest to the left exploded.

Dirt and rocks blew up in the faces of the startled men and horses, killing two of them instantly.

Drifter aimed and fired, exploding another stick of dynamite. The explosion killed several more Comancheros as well as their horses, one of them thrashing and screaming before it died.

Emily fired again. Missed. Levered in another round, aimed, and fired. The fiery explosion forced the remaining Comancheros to withdraw, but not before Drifter exploded the fourth stick, killing three more men.

'Keep firing,' he told Emily. 'Doesn't matter what you hit, man or horse, just keep pumping lead into 'em. If we're lucky maybe we can chase them off.'

She obeyed, her steady firing causing havoc among the retreating riders.

Drifter kept pace with her, his deadly accuracy chasing the Comancheros back to the foothills.

'I'm out,' Emily said, holding up her rifle.

Drifter pulled his last few rounds from his pocket and tossed them to her.

'Reload but hold your fire,' he said. 'I'm almost out too. When they come at us again, we need to make every round count.'

'Maybe they won't come again.'

'Always that chance,' Drifter agreed.

She saw his face and knew he was lying for her sake.

'I won't forget to save one round,' she said bravely.

'Don't worry. It won't come to that.' He hid his fears behind a smile, having already decided that he'd shoot her himself before he let her fall into the Comancheros' hands.

Emily looked at Cordero, still seated astride the pack mule, then back at Drifter. 'You won't let him live, will you?'

'Not a chance.'

Relieved, Emily thanked him, adding: 'I know I won't go to heaven for wishing him dead, but I don't care. He's—'

Drifter stopped her. 'Emily—'

'Yes?'

He hesitated and looked toward the foothills. The remaining dozen or so Comancheros were milling around, brandishing their weapons as they pumped themselves up for another charge.

'What were you going to say?' she asked.

He knew he should tell her the truth, but he couldn't. He flat out couldn't.

'Wasn't important,' he said. 'Just wanted to, you know, say—' He stopped as he heard the Comancheros yelling and, turning his head, saw they were once again charging toward them.

'Remember,' he said grimly. 'Make every shot count.'

She nodded, rested her rifle atop the rocks, and took careful aim.

Drifter drew his Colt, spun the cylinder to make sure it was full and then set the gun on the rock, ready to use once his rifle was empty.

They came in fast, all thirteen of them, yelling, pumping their rifles, easily visible in the pale moonlight, the dust from their horses' hoofs swirling up around them like a shroud of doom.

Emily fired first, her shot knocking the lead rider from his horse. Drifter fired, picking off a second rider. Both of them fired again, but this time only one horse went down, pitching its rider over its head.

The Comancheros were now less than fifty yards away, some of them firing as they rode. Bullets chipped at the rocks about Drifter and Emily's heads, forcing them briefly to duck down.

Then they started firing again. But though they hit several riders, only one went down. The rest kept coming and Drifter could hear *El Carnicero* laughing behind him. He fired once more then ran out of ammo. Discarding the rifle, he grabbed his Colt and fired into the onrushing riders.

Beside him Emily also ran out of ammo and looked helplessly at him.

Nine Comancheros remained alive and they were now less than thirty yards away.

Drifter fired twice, killing a rider each time. Then as the other seven men continued to charge toward them, he turned and aimed his gun at Emily, ready to shoot her.

She closed her eyes and lowered her head, unable to face him.

He started to squeeze the trigger, when a shot rang out, followed rapidly by four more shots, each one knocking a rider from his saddle.

Surprised, Drifter turned from Emily and looked at the Comancheros. Only two remained and they had reined up, equally shocked by the deadly shooting, and were now spurring their horses off across the scrubland.

They didn't get far.

In front of the hills a tall man sat astride a motionless, magnificent coal-black Morgan stallion, rifle couched against his shoulder, sights trained on the two Comancheros desperately trying to gallop out of range.

Two shots were fired.

Two riders pitched from their saddles.

Two riderless horses slowed and then stopped, reins trailing in the dirt.

Then it was over.

Drifter could only shake his head and grin.

'I . . . I thought he was dead,' Emily said.

'Me too,' said Drifter. 'But Gabe, he's one hard *hombre* to kill.'

Emily got to her feet, half-laughing, half-crying with relief.

'I was so s-scared,' she said, moving close to Drifter.

'Me too,' he said. He put his arms around her, all awkwardness gone, and held her against him. She began to sob and he could feel her heart thudding against his chest. He felt the sting of his eyes moistening and then a feeling of overwhelming joy flooded through him.

He heard a horse trotting toward them. Looking up, he rested his chin atop Emily's head and watched as Mesquite Jennings rode up.

'Sure took your damn sweet time,' Drifter said to him.

The outlaw grinned. 'Can blame that on Brandy. Sonofagun kept tryin' to buck me off as we rode down the mountain.'

'Where's Sheriff Forbes?'

Mesquite shook his head, indicating Forbes was dead. Then before Drifter or Emily could say anything, he looked off at something, adding: 'You gonna just let him ride away like that?'

Drifter turned and saw *El Carnicero* riding off on the pack mule. The animal was moving slowly, reluctantly, despite Cordero's desperate urging, and Drifter let go of Emily and gestured for Mesquite to throw him his rifle.

'Don't,' Emily said as Drifter went to shoot. 'He's mine.'

Before Drifter could argue, she quickly mounted and

rode after Cordero.

'Let her go,' Mesquite said as Drifter started to mount up. 'If anybody's got a right to kill someone, it's her.'

'It's not the killing I'm worried about,' Drifter said. 'It's her having to live with it afterward.'

'That ain't gonna happen,' Mesquite said. He crooked one leg around his saddle-horn and lazily thumbed in Emily's direction.

Drifter looked over the sorrel's neck and saw Emily leading the pack mule back toward them ... an enraged and frustrated Cordero cursing her from its back.

CHAPTER TWENTY-SEVEN

'I've decided I want him to hang,' Emily told Drifter and Mesquite as they herded the mares across the open scrubland in the direction of the Devil's Furnace. 'I want to take him back to Santa Rosa and have him tried, sentenced and then hanged for murdering my family.' She paused and looked back at *El Carnicero* who stared fixedly ahead as he rode behind Drifter. 'I know it probably won't feel as good as pulling the trigger myself, but I got to thinking about it and I knew it's what Pa would want me to do.'

'Wise decision,' Drifter said. 'Once you've killed someone there's no going back, and it leaves an ugly taste in your mouth for the rest of your life.'

'Is that how you feel?' Emily asked Mesquite.

'All the time,' he lied.

'I'm glad,' she said. 'People in Santa Rosa say you're nothing but a gunfighter, cold-blooded as they come, but I knew you weren't first time I met you.'

Mesquite looked at Drifter, who rolled his eyes. 'Just goes to show you,' he said cheerfully. 'Even decent folks can make a mistake.' Not wanting to dig himself a deeper hole he reined in a little, slowing the cantankerous Morgan so that the stallion fell back alongside the mule carrying Cordero.

139

They rode on. Overhead, dawn was flooding the pale lavender sky with streaks of gold and crimson. Already the air was warming and heat was rising from the ground. In the distance sunlight pierced the thinning clouds, the rays reflecting off the flat, glaring white sand of *El Horno del Diablo*. Potential death awaited them and presently Drifter called a halt and said that unless anyone had any objections, he thought they should rest up during the day at the same place they'd rested before, then eat something and ride on to Blanco Canyon that night.

'Suits me,' Mesquite said. 'But I reckon you ought to know: once we're clear of *del Diablo*, I'll be ridin' south.'

'How so?' Drifter asked, surprised.

'Well, now that Forbes ain't sheriff no longer, the folks in Santa Rosa will insist El Paso send a deputy US marshal to keep the peace till they can elect a new one. And you know who they'll send?'

'Ezra Macahan?'

Mesquite nodded.

'I've heard of him,' Emily put in. 'Pa said he was the best lawman west of St Louis.'

'An' the most stubborn,' Mesquite grumbled. 'Step on that fella's shadow an' he'll hunt you to your grave.'

'So you're gonna hole up down here till a sheriff's elected?' Drifter asked.

'Yep. Way I figure it, the new tin star will be so busy shakin' hands and kissin' babies, he won't have no time to round up posses or hunt me down.'

Drifter didn't say anything, though he was clearly disappointed. He knew that trying to get Emily, the mares, and Cordero safely through Blanco Canyon even *with* Mesquite's help would be a daunting task; without him, it was plain suicidal.

Sensing his dilemma Emily said: 'Isn't there *any* way around it?'

Mesquite shrugged. 'None I know of.'

'We'll make it,' Drifter said, not too convincingly. 'We got through once, we'll do it again.' They rode on in gloomy silence.

CHAPTER TWENTY-EIGHT

They lost one of the mares while crossing the desert. A slate-colored grullo named Nina, she was fine-boned and more highly strung than the others and faded in the oppressing heat faster than they did. Several times she stumbled as they plodded across the burning sand and though Emily rode alongside her, encouraging her when she seemed ready to drop, finally her last drop of stamina ran out and she collapsed. Nor would she rise when Emily quickly dismounted, tipped some water into the mare's foaming mouth, and then tried to drag her to her feet.

'Leave her be,' Drifter said.

'No, no, she just needs to rest so she can get her strength back.'

'Dammit, Emily, we can't stop. Not in this heat.'

'Then you go ahead,' she said stubbornly. 'I'll catch up with you.'

'Absolutely not.'

Emily grabbed his reins, pleading: 'Please, Quint . . . I can't just leave her here to die.'

A shot rang out. The mare grunted and went limp.

Emily whirled and saw Mesquite returning his Colt to its holster.

'Y-you beast!' she hissed at him.

Mesquite ignored her, tapped his heels against the Morgan's ribs and moved off.

'Cool off,' Drifter told Emily. 'The man did you a favor. Now, get yourself in that saddle and ride, or you're gonna lose more than horses to this heat.'

Furious and near tears, she nevertheless obeyed him. But angry at the world, she wouldn't ride beside him or Mesquite, instead falliing in alongside her mares.

El Horno del Diablo had claimed another victim!

It was mid-morning when they finally reached the sandy hollow circled by boulders where they had previously slept. Everyone was too drained and exhausted to talk. After driving the mares inside the horseshoe-shaped area, Drifter and Mesquite tied their ropes across the entrance and then unsaddled their horses before spreading their bedrolls under the large overhanging rock.

Lastly, Drifter untied Cordero's feet, helped him off the mule and led him to the shade cast by the rock. There, he gave him a sip of water and then tied his hands and feet with the same piece of rope.

El Carnicero sneered at him. 'Do not worry, *gringo*. Now is not the time to escape. But when we come to Blanco Canyon. . . .' Leaving the rest unsaid, he closed his eyes and leaned back against the rock.

Drifter left him and joined Mesquite, who was wiping the Morgan's lips with a wet kerchief.

'Keep an eye on Cordero while I go pull up the last of the shin-daggers. With these mares to water, we need every drop we can suck out of them.'

' 'Fore you do that,' Mesquite said. 'Why don't you tell Emily the truth?'

' 'Bout what?'

'Who you really are. Don't act the innocent whore with

143

me,' he added when Drifter pretended to look puzzled. 'This damn fool charade has gone on long enough. It's time to come clean. I mean, look at her. Poor kid couldn't be more depressed if she tried.'

'Why wouldn't she be?' Drifter said angrily. 'All the hell she's gone through lately. On top of that, though she hasn't said anything, I know she blames herself for Sheriff Forbes's death and the loss of her pa's stallion. And now, a few hours ago, you shoot one of her mares. Jesus on the cross, Gabe, what the hell do you expect from the kid – a song and dance?'

'I don't expect *nothin'* from her! It's you I'm talkin' about. You'n that damn debt you keep sayin' you owe her.'

'What I owe Emily is none of your goddamn business!'

'I'm makin' it my business.'

Drifter frowned and wiped his nose with his fist. 'Why?'

'Let's just say I like her.' He glanced at Emily, who lay on her blanket, arms folded behind her head, staring glumly at the rock a few feet above her face. 'She's got sand. Reminds me of how Cally used to be. Not afraid to spit in the wind. Now,' he said when Drifter didn't respond, 'you gonna belly up to the bar or wait for me to tell her?'

Drifter stiffened. For a moment it appeared as if he might hit Mesquite, might even go for his gun; but then reason prevailed and his anger faded. Giving a long weary sigh, he said: 'How'd you find out?'

'Rumors. Gossip. Folks talk, you hear things.'

'Yet you never said anything? Not even when I told you I was following her?'

'I wasn't sure. Not till I saw the way you looked at her in Palomas. How protective you were of her. Then I knew.' Pausing, he looked at Emily with genuine affection before adding: 'I'll make you a deal, Quint. You tell her now an' I'll help you get through Blanco Canyon.'

Drifter studied him shrewdly. 'Blackmail?'

144

' "A rose by any other name", as Cally always used to say.'

Drifter chuckled despite himself. Then releasing all his pent-up emotions in one long painful sigh, he turned and walked over to Emily.

CHAPTER TWENTY-NINE

She didn't look at him as he ducked in under the rock and sat beside her.

Stomach knotted by anxiety, he cleared his throat and had to swallow several times before he could say: 'Emily . . . 'bout the mare. I'm truly sorry but . . . there wasn't anything you could have done that would've saved her.'

Her parched lips tightened into a thin white line and she continued staring at the rock above her. 'You could've at least let me try.'

'No. In this heat and with a lack of water that would've been irresponsible. And being a leader means being responsible. Surely you can see that?'

She said only: 'I thought you were my friend.'

It was the opening he'd been looking for. 'I am your friend,' he said gently. 'But I'm also a . . . lot more.'

Something in his voice made her rise up on her elbows and look at him. 'What're you talking about?'

Drifter hesitated, fear of rejection blocking the words he so badly wanted to say. He'd been in gunfights and battled Apaches and never once had his mouth gone dry. Now his mouth felt furry and parched, and he had to bring up spittle before he could talk. 'Emily, what I'm going to say . . .

well, it'll come as a shock and might hurt you ... might even make you angry. ...'

She frowned, surprised. 'Why?'

He tried to meet her steady brown gaze, but couldn't.

'Because ... in some ways it'll take something away from you, something you loved and ... treasured.'

'Then why tell me?'

' 'Cause I'm hoping at the same time it will help you; stop you from feeling so alone and ... lonely.'

'I don't understand.'

'Not sure I do myself. Not even sure if telling you is the right thing. I mean, I've wanted to tell you for a long but I couldn't.'

'Why not?'

'I promised your mother I wouldn't.'

'Momma? What's she got to do with it?'

'Everything. If I hadn't given her my word, she wouldn't have let me come by the ranch every once in a while to see you.'

'But you and Pa are – were friends.'

'That's another reason I couldn't tell you.'

'Tell me what?' Emily began. Then before he could answer: 'Wait a minute. Does this have to do with how she felt about you? That's it, isn't it?' Momma loved you, didn't she? And you ... you loved her?'

Drifter closed his eyes for a moment, trying to shut out the past; those years of painful loneliness, of drifting from ranch to ranch asking strangers for work, when the only place he really wanted to be was with the woman he loved, the woman who loved him but was sharing the bed of another man; her husband, a fine man, a man he, Quint, admired, and a man who also loved her and probably, all things considered, deserved her more than he did.

Emily's voice interrupted his thoughts. 'Well, answer me,' he heard her say. 'Did you love my mother?'

'Yes,' he said finally. 'Very much.'

'And that's what you've wanted to tell me all these years?'

'That and . . . look,' he said, interrupting himself. 'What I've really wanted to tell you, but couldn't because it not only meant breaking my promise but would've hurt everyone – me, you, your mother and father, brothers – *everyone*! And that was the last thing I wanted.'

'Then why are you telling me now?'

'Because now things are different. Now you have no one and I—' He paused as his courage suddenly deserted him; then, as she stared up at him, her lovely dark eyes filled with sadness, he blurted out: 'Emily . . . I'm your father.'

Her mouth dropped and her brows arched, more in disbelief than surprise. 'B-but that's impossible! Momma once told me how babies are born and—' It hit her then and, in a flash, anger replaced her disbelief and surprise.

'I don't believe you!' she exclaimed. 'Momma would never do a hateful, mean thing like that. Not to Pa. Not even if she loved you.'

'I'm sorry,' Drifter said, not knowing what else to say. 'I wish to God it weren't true but—'

Suddenly she attacked him, fists balled, punching him in the chest and the face, sobbing, and at the same time spitting with rage. 'I hate you! *Hate* you! *Hate you*!'

He made no attempt to stop her; to protect himself from her blows. He just sat there, silently, passively taking it, until finally someone grabbed her from behind and dragged her out from under the overhanging rock.

'Stop it! *Stop it*! You hear me, Emily? Cut it out! That's enough!' Mesquite bear-hugged her so that she couldn't move anything but her legs.

'Let me go!' she screamed, kicking. 'Let me go . . . lemme go!'

'Settle down an' I will,' he promised. She fought him for a few more moments and then, powerless, finally went limp in his arms.

Drifter ducked out from under the overhang and joined Mesquite.

'It's all right,' he said quietly. 'Put her down.'

Mesquite obeyed, gently setting Emily on her feet.

She stood there, chest heaving, eyes blazing, glaring at both of them.

'I'll never talk to you again,' she hissed to Drifter. 'Never ever!' She stormed off.

They watched as she marched over to where the mares stood passively in the broiling sun and slumped down with her back against a boulder.

'That went well,' Mesquite said.

'My fault,' Drifter said. 'I never should have told her. Should've realized how she'd take it. She's only fourteen, for chrissake. Hell, under the circumstances it's a goddamn miracle she's even holding herself together.'

'Quit beatin' on yourself, hoss. You done the right thing. An' after she's calmed down an' had time to chew on it, she'll feel the same way. Most likely say she's sorry an' ask you to forgive her . . . then you two can get together an' start lovin' each other like you should've all along.'

He walked off leaving Drifter standing there in the sweltering sun, feeling as if he'd just made the biggest mistake of his life.

CHAPTER THIRTY

True to her word Emily did not speak to Drifter as the four of them – *El Carnicero* once more astride the pack mule – rode across the Devil's Furnace in the cool moonlit darkness. She didn't say much to Mesquite either, but instead concentrated on keeping the mares together and not allowing any of them to stop, even for a moment.

They rode until dawn lightened the eastern sky behind a far-off mountain range. By then they could make out the ominous pinkish-white cliffs that formed the entrance to Blanco Canyon. Calling a halt, Drifter joined Mesquite for a smoke while they tried to figure out the best way to outwit the *bandidos*.

'Maybe we can make a swap?' Mesquite said. 'Our lives for his?'

Knowing he was referring to Cordero, Drifter looked dubious. 'Why would they trade for something they'll get anyway once they've killed us?'

'You always were an optimistic bastard,' Mesquite grumbled.

'Facing facts is *realistic*, not pessimistic, especially since we only have thirty rounds between us. Anyway, you know better than to make deals with bandits. Second we turned him over they'd slit our throats and then take turns abusing Emily.'

Mesquite scowled at the idea, then glanced her way, saying: 'How long you think she'll go not talkin' to you?'

'I wouldn't want to be hanging by my fingertips from a cliff waiting until she did,' Drifter said grimly.

Mesquite shrugged and flipped his smoke away. 'Then it's settled, *amigo*. We meet this scum head-on an' hope we're the last ones standin'!'

'Hope,' Drifter growled. 'Now there's a word to build your dreams on.'

Over an hour had passed by the time they reached the mouth of Blanco Canyon. By now the sun had cleared the mountains, but still wasn't high enough to shed light on the narrow trail that curved, snake-like, through the towering sandstone cliffs.

Mesquite and Emily herded the mares ahead of them, while Drifter brought up the rear, Winchester across his saddle, left hand gripping the reins of the pack mule carrying Cordero. The Comancheros' leader was bound and gagged so he couldn't alert the bandits, and his feet were still tied together by a rope that looped under the horse's belly.

As they rode slowly around one curve after another, Drifter and Mesquite kept their eyes trained on the upper walls of the canyon, where natural caves and fissures in the rocks offered ideal hiding places for snipers. Twice Drifter glimpsed what he thought was someone moving along the top of the cliffs. Both times it was followed by a dribbling of dirt and shale, and though nothing came of it he called out to Mesquite and Emily, warning them to be on the alert for rockslides.

They were halfway through the canyon, and Drifter was teasing himself with the possibility that maybe the bandits were not going to attack, when suddenly, after rounding a bend, they were confronted by a barricade of rocks. Five feet high, it stretched from one wall to the other, blocking their escape.

A dozen *bandidos* crouched behind the barricade, rifles aimed at Drifter and Mesquite, while their new leader, Agapita Muñoz, a squat, shabbily-dressed man with a high-crowned sombrero and two pearl-handled *pistolas* in his belt, contemptuously eyed them from an overhanging ledge.

'*Buenos días, yanquis,*' he said mockingly. 'It is good you come this way again. My men, they are eager to repay you for the death of *Jefe* Baca.'

Mesquite grinned wolfishly. 'And you, *hombre*, what's your stake in this?'

'*Adolfito era mi primo.*'

'Your cousin, huh?' Mesquite turned to Drifter. 'Hear that, Gabe? I shot this poor fella's cousin.'

'It's a real tragedy,' Drifter deadpanned. 'You ought to be ashamed of yourself.' Then, sobering, he said to Muñoz: 'We don't want to have to shoot any more of your cousins. So why don't you roll some of those rocks away and let us ride on through peacefully?'

Muñoz smiled, showing a single gold front tooth glinting in a mouthful of broken, rotted ones. 'My men, they would not let me do this thing you ask.'

'Then you'll be the first to die,' Mesquite said sweetly.

Muñoz considered his fate for a moment, then said: 'If I agree, *gringo*, you must give us your horses.'

'Mean my apology ain't enough?' Mesquite said.

Muñoz lost his smile and his hands inched toward his pistols.

Emily said quickly: '*Por favor, señor* – would you take gold instead?'

Muñoz and his men immediately became interested. 'You have gold, *señorita?*'

'No,' Drifter said before Emily could reply. 'No gold!'

'*No hay oro?*'

'No.'

'But the *señorita*, she say—'

'She's mixed up . . .' Drifter pointed at the sun and twirled his finger next to his head, suggesting Emily wasn't all there. '*Es el calor. Demasiado sol.*'

'He means the sun's scrambled her brains,' Mesquite said cheerfully.

Muñoz eyed Mesquite and Drifter suspiciously, then turned to his men and said mockingly: '*Los gringos dicen que la señorita esta loca.*'

The *bandidos* doubled over with laughter. '*Sí . . . sí . . . está loca.*'

Emily gestured to Muñoz, '*Un momento, por favor,*' and dismounted.

'Emily,' Drifter barked, 'get back on your horse!' Then as she ignored him: 'Now, goddammit!'

Again she ignored him. Reaching under the cantle of her saddle, she pulled out a small leather pouch, held it up to Muñoz and jiggled it, saying: '*Oro, señor. Mucho oro!*'

Muñoz beamed as he heard clinking inside the pouch.

'Aww, shit,' Mesquite said. He rolled his eyes and went for his gun.

Drifter did the same and aimed his Colt at Muñoz.

Instantly, the bandits behind the barricade raised their rifles, ready to fire.

'No, no!' Emily cried. 'Don't shoot! Don't shoot!' Hurrying to one of the mares, she looped the string attached to the pouch over its head, shouting: '*Mucho oro! Mucho oro!*'

The mare, frightened by her shouting, reared up, whinnying and pawing at the air and then bolted. At once the other mares panicked. They scattered and blocked by the barricade, galloped back along the canyon.

Immediately, the bandits began hollering at each other,

then at Muñoz. And before he could stop them, they had scrambled over the barricade and were chasing after the mares.

Muñoz hesitated; then after a helpless shrug at Drifter and Mesquite he ran after his men.

Drifter glared at Emily, who hadn't moved. 'Dammit, girl, you gave me your word!'

'I didn't disobey you,' she said. 'They were *my* mares. If I want to give them away, I can!'

Mesquite said grimly: 'A good man died for those mares, Emily – a man I didn't even have time to bury. Too bad you didn't think of that.'

'I *did* think of that,' she said. 'In fact I've *been* thinking about it ever since we left the hills. That's why I did it.'

'Did what?' Drifter said.

'Saved our lives.' She reached inside her shirt and pulled out a small cloth bag. Opening it, she took out a handful of twenty dollar gold pieces. 'Much as I wanted those mares, I couldn't have any more deaths on my conscience.'

It took a moment for it to dawn on Drifter and Mesquite, then they cracked up.

'W-what was in the pouch?' Drifter asked.

'Stones,' Emily said. 'I made the swap when we stopped at the lava bed.'

'Emily,' Mesquite said, wiping his eyes, 'you are a treat.'

'But now you don't have the mares or your stallion,' Drifter said.

'It's all right,' she said, indicating *El Carnicero*, 'I've got him. That's more important than any horse alive!' Mounting, she kicked her horse into a gallop and rode straight at the barricade.

Drifter and Mesquite watched, alarmed, as a collision appeared imminent. But at the last instant Emily shouted encouragement to her horse and both animal and rider soared over the barricade. Landing safely on the other side, she reined up and waved for Drifter and Mesquite to follow.

Both men stared at her with a mixture of surprise and admiration.

Then, 'Yep,' said Drifter. 'That's my daughter all right.' Dismounting, he led the sorrel to the barricade and began rolling rocks aside so they could pass through.

CHAPTER
THIRTY-ONE

The closer they got to Palomas, the stronger the wind became.

Los fuertes vientos, as strong winds were known, were not uncommon in the region. But this wind, which arrived with the dawn, was especially potent: a powerful howling force that swept in from the hills and stormed across the scrubland, filling the hot, dry air with stinging sand, ripping signs from the ramshackle stores and cantinas in Palomas, and turning the sky a dull, reddish tan.

On entering town Drifter, Emily and Mesquite, hats jammed on their heads, kerchiefs covering their faces, bodies hunched forward over the necks of their horses, saw that the streets were deserted and realized that in one way, the wind had done them a favor: it had driven everyone indoors. With any luck they would be able to buy more ammo and then be on their way before any of the local riff-raff could try to rob or kill them.

Unable to be heard above the wind, Drifter pointed at the ochre-colored adobe building that housed the general store. Emily and Mesquite nodded to show they understood and nudged their horses in that direction. Drifter led the pack mule carrying Cordero to the hitch-rail, then dis-

156

mounted and handed the lead-rope and his reins to Emily. 'We'll only be a few minutes,' he promised. 'If anyone gives you any trouble, including him' – he nodded at Cordero, who sat, hands tied, motionless beneath his sombrero – 'fire a shot.'

'With what?' she replied.

'Here,' Mesquite tossed her his Winchester. 'Use this.' He followed Drifter into the store.

Emily rose up in the stirrups to ease her cramped thighs and buttocks, then settled back down in the saddle and squinted about her. The wind raged. It rattled windows and tore off a shutter, sending it cartwheeling down the street. Sand stung Emily's cheeks above her kerchief and tugged at her hat. She pulled it down harder on her head. She could hear a bell ringing, its herky-jerky clanging muffled by the wind, and she remembered the little church they'd passed on their way in.

Thinking of the church reminded her of Sundays, of going to prayer meetings or to church with her family, kneeling in the pew alongside her brothers, offering thanks to God, and trying not to fall asleep during Father Mateo's long-winded sermons. For a moment she saw the faces of her mother, father, and brothers and a surge of happiness flooded through her. Then the faces vanished, leaving empty holes in her heart. Never again, she thought. Never. Ever. Again. Tears welled into her eyes. She blinked them away and angrily looked sideways at Cordero. She found him staring fixedly at her, his dark eyes filled with murderous hate.

Hanging's too good for you, she thought. *I want you to die slowly, to rot in a filthy prison cell full of rats for the rest of your miserable life.* Instantly, she chided herself for harboring such evil thoughts and tried hard to find forgiveness in her heart for the Comancheros' leader. It was impossible. Ashamed, she begged God's forgiveness and promised herself that from

157

now on she would leave *El Carnicero*'s fate in His hands.

It was then a sudden gale-like gust of wind struck her like a giant invisible punch – almost pushing her from the saddle. Startled, she saved herself by grabbing the pommel with one hand, the mane of her horse with the other. At the same instant a bouncing tumbleweed ricocheted off the hitch-rail and struck her horse in the face. Panicked, it reared up snorting, unseating Emily who fell to the ground. She landed flat on her back. Stunned, she didn't see her horse rear up again, this time lashing out with its front hoofs and striking the pack mule on the neck. It, too, reared up, stumbled, lost its balance in the buffeting wind, and went down hard.

The next thing Emily remembered, she was cradled in Drifter's arms and he was saying something she couldn't hear above the wind. Finally, she realized he was asking her if she was all right. She nodded, 'Y-yes, yes . . . I'm fine,' and with his help struggled to her feet. Squinting, she saw the pack mule standing nearby. Its legs were trembling, the saddle was empty and the mule was coated in dirt as if it had rolled in the street. Mesquite stood beside it, re-fastening the straps that held all their gear.

'W-where's *El Carnicero*?' she asked. 'Did he escape?'

Drifter shrugged. 'Only a rope,' he said laconically. He stepped back so she could see Cordero's corpse sprawled in the dirt behind him.

'Oh my God,' she cried. 'What happened?'

'Neck's busted. Must've happened when the mule went down. Either rolled over on him or kicked him as it tried to get up. Hard to know for sure.'

'Don't matter anyway,' Mesquite said. 'Bastard's dead; that's all that counts. We ought to get out of here,' he added. 'This wind dies down we could be lookin' at a rope ourselves.'

Drifter rested a hand on Emily's shoulder. 'Think you can ride?' he asked, concerned.

'Sure. Honestly, Quint, I'm fine.' Stepping into the saddle, she gave Cordero's corpse a final bitter look and silently thanked God for answering her prayer. 'Let's leave him here,' she said. 'He and this town deserve each other.'

Leaving *El Carnicero*'s body propped up against the wall of a cantina, his face covered with his sombrero as if he were sleeping, they rode out of town.

After a mile or so heading north, the wind slackened. They lowered their kerchiefs and dusted themselves off. The US border now lay less than a mile away.

Mesquite dismounted, tipped water from his canteen on to his kerchief and gently rubbed away the sand caked around the stallion's eyes. For his trouble, Brandy tried to bite him. Mesquite jumped back, avoiding the Morgan's teeth and slapped the horse with his hat. 'Damn you,' he said, exasperated. 'Don't know why I don't put a round between your eyes right now.'

Drifter chuckled. 'For the same reason I don't shoot Wilson, here: we need them.'

Mesquite snorted in disgust, and then swung up into the saddle. 'Well, here's where I dust you two off.'

Crestfallen, Emily said: 'Wish you'd change your mind; come with us.'

'Maybe next time,' he said. 'But I'll sorely miss you.'

'Miss you too,' Emily said. Then: 'Am I ever going to see you again?'

' 'Course. Next time I ride up to see Ingrid, I'll swing by the ranch and say hidee.'

'But I'm selling the ranch. Going back to school.'

'No sweat. I'll track you down somehow. That's a promise. 'Sides,' he said, looking at Drifter, 'you'll know where she is, right?'

'At all times,' Drifter said, adding: 'that's if she still wants me around.'

'I don't have a choice,' Emily deadpanned. 'You're all I've got.'

'Thanks.' Drifter rolled his eyes at Mesquite. 'Sure you don't want to take her off my hands?'

Mesquite laughed then wheeled the all-black Morgan around. '*Adios, mis amigos,*' he said and rode off, heading south across the sun-baked flatland.

Emily waved and blew him a kiss. '*Vaya con Dios,*' she called after him.

A little later, when she and Drifter were riding toward the border crossing at Columbus, she said: 'He was just saying that, wasn't he? About tracking me down, I mean?'

'No,' Drifter said. 'Gabe's got his faults, like the rest of us, but breaking his word isn't one of them.'

'I'm glad,' Emily said. 'I really like him.'

Drifter smiled and rubbed his nose with his fist. 'You're not the first woman to feel that way. And sure as the sun comes up, you won't be the last.'